D0166602

FINLEY PIKE

AND THE SODD

For Curtis—You're very wonderful

FINLEY PIKE
AND THE SODD

ANNELIESE RIDER

1

FINLEY DIDN'T WANT to sit down. She didn't care about tides, science class, or grumpy old Mr. Slinch, who was repeating himself for the third time.

"Sit down, Finley. This is your last warning before I send you to detention." She was opening her mouth to tell him she didn't care about detention when someone kicked her leg. It was Dale. She frowned, but reluctantly sat. Mr. Slinch hadn't seen the kick. He smiled smugly. "Thank you."

Finley slumped in her chair. When Mr. Slinch turned his back, Dale slipped her a note.

You can't get detention today. Remember our plan?

He was right. They wouldn't have time for their adventure if she had to spend an extra hour at school.

She started talking to Dale last week when Mr. Slinch made them partners for an assignment. Dale was fun, adventurous, and kind. Finley didn't want to miss the chance

9

to go exploring with him—especially where they planned to go today.

But Mr. Slinch had threatened her with detention three times and the morning wasn't even half over. It was going to be a long day. Despair set into the pit of Finley's stomach. She'd started off the year excited for high school, hoping it would be better than middle school.

So far, it wasn't.

She made it through the rest of the morning by staring at the second button on Mr. Slinch's shirt, but after lunch everything fell apart. Mrs. O'Malley left the classroom for a few minutes to go to the office, and Finley was walking to her desk when Rusty Cowell tripped her. She went tumbling down to the dirty speckled brown carpet.

Rusty, the Malvern Middle School bully, was in ninth grade now, and he was trying to continue his reign of terror.

Sprawled on the floor and listening to Rusty laugh, something snapped and Finley's mind went crimson. As she leaped to her feet, someone groaned—it was Dale, watching their adventure dissolve before his eyes. Finley grabbed Rusty's shirt front and screamed,

"Rusty Cowell, I HATE YOU!"

Then, balling her small hands into fists, she hit him in the chest again and again. The class watched in amazement. They'd never seen anyone stand up to Rusty at the middle school. For the past few years, he'd ruled his grade with brawn and no brains, and no one tried to stop him. He picked on Finley in middle school, but he'd gotten much worse since this school year had started. Rusty growled a threat between Finley's wild swings.

"If you don't stop, I'll steal your lunch every day for the rest of the year." She didn't stop. He repeated himself several times and half-heartedly swung back at her, but his voice slowly lost conviction as she continued. Trying another tactic, he taunted, "When are you going to start hitting me? It doesn't even hurt."

Finley appeared to hear him this time, and she slammed her fists into him with renewed vigor. Soon he stopped grinning and started whimpering.

Finley's fist was in midair when someone behind her cleared his throat. The principal! She paused, then decided to make it worth it, since she was already in trouble. Redirecting her aim, she planted a fist on Rusty's nose. He let out a yell as a large hand gently pulled Finley back.

She was probably going to get detention for a year. Maybe she would get suspended. Or expelled. Last year in eighth grade, Bobby Jones climbed out the second story window and was suspended for a week. Fighting was worse than climbing out a window.

Turning slowly, she found herself staring into compassionate brown eyes. It wasn't the principal, it was a tall man in a green plaid shirt and dirty khaki pants, with a huge ring of keys on his belt. Finley didn't know who he was. She looked up at him in meek silence, while Rusty started into a sing-song whine.

"She hit me. Didn't you all see that?" Blood trickled from his nostrils, and he looked around at his classmates. Other students always sided with Rusty—no one wanted to risk getting beat to a pulp after school, which was his classic threat. He continued, "I was minding my own business and she attacked me."

But the class remained silent, torn between fear of Rusty and admiration for someone who would stand up to him.

The tall man looked at Rusty, and his whimpering subsided.

"Go to the bathroom and take care of that nose." Rusty looked at him in disbelief, and the man added, "That wasn't a request."

Rusty shuffled out, holding a tissue on his nose and mumbling about injustice. The huge man picked up Finley's book, pointed her to her empty chair, and walked to the front of the class. He said,

"Mrs. O'Malley asked me to check on you."

He'd heard the whole episode as he walked up to the door of her class. He knew from seeing them around school that Rusty Cowell was a coward and a bully, and that Finley Pike had more energy and emotions than she knew how to handle. He stared at the class. The class stared back.

Finally a girl raised her hand.

"Excuse me, mister . . . but who are you?"

The skin around his eyes creased into pleasant wrinkles as he smiled.

"Michell Fitzwell."

The girl wasn't satisfied.

"What do you do?"

"I'm a magician."

His eyes sparkled as the class considered this in dead silence. Before anyone could react, they heard Mrs. O'Malley's shoes clicking in the hallway. Mitchell Fitzwell nodded amiably and walked out. The hurried whispers flew. One kid said,

"Did you see his hands? They were the size of basketballs!"

Another girl leaned forward to her friend.

"He was at least seven feet tall."

A third said,

"I think he might have cast a spell on Rusty. Maybe he'll turn into a frog."

And a fourth answered,

"What if he cast a spell on *all of us*?"

When Mrs. O'Malley walked in, the class fell silent. Rusty wasn't poking the girl in front of him with pencils, the girls in the front row weren't whispering, and not a single boy in the back row was sleeping.

"Did Mr. Fitzwell cast a spell on you or something?" The class stared at her in terror, but Finley just stared at her hands. Mrs. O'Malley raised an eyebrow.

2

FINLEY WAITED ALL day for the dreaded intercom to summon her to the office—but it never did. When the last bell rang, she scooped everything from her desk into her backpack and rushed out into the late September afternoon.

She'd agreed to meet Dale at the skate park after dropping off her stuff. At home, Steve, her mom's boyfriend, was sitting at the kitchen table holding a glass of orange juice, eyes half-closed.

"Hi Steve, did mom go shopping yesterday?"

He swung his head toward her and squinted.

"Farley? No."

"It's Finley."

Steve shook his head as if trying to clear fog.

"Oh yeah. Spindley Finley."

Amused, he guffawed. Finley cringed. All of her mom's boyfriends had different habits. The first one she remembered was Joe. He'd been her favorite because he sometimes gave her candy. Then Rex, who yelled all the time and burned everything he tried to cook. But at least he tried to cook. Ron came next, but when he started stealing money from her mom's wallet, she dumped him. There were a few more before Steve, but her grandpa called them all "Good-for-nothings." When Steve moved in, Finley asked,

"Are you a good-for-nothing, too?"

He'd just laughed.

Almost every time he saw her he made up a different nickname for her. He always thought it was very funny, but Finley didn't. She opened the fridge. It was empty. The pantry was too, besides some random odds and ends, like dried beans and onion soup mix. Hurrying into her bedroom, Finley put on her favorite bright pink pants and a dingy white t-shirt. Her stomach growled as she pulled the shirt over her head.

When she got to Dale's house, his mom answered the door. Finley introduced herself. Mrs. Kellogg said,

"Yes, Dale told me about you. It's nice to meet you. Dale's already on his way to the park."

Finley nodded and stood there a moment longer. Mrs. Kellogg smiled sweetly, and Finley decided it was worth asking.

"Can I have a snack?"

Mrs. Kellogg had guessed from the little that Dale told her about Finley that her home life wasn't easy. She immediately said,

"Of course! I'll be right back."

She returned with an apple, a cheese stick, and a small bag of crackers. Finley thanked her and took off. Dale was sitting on the picnic table at the park when Finley arrived, out of breath from her run down Main Street. She sat down and bit into the apple.

"That's what my snack was today too!"

Finley nodded.

"I stopped at your house."

"Oh."

"I met your mom. She's nice."

"Cool."

As Finley chomped on her apple, they discussed their plan. While walking home from the library one day last week, Dale noticed the door to the abandoned jewelry store on Main Street was wide open, so he went in and looked around. When he told Finley about it, she'd begged to see. He agreed to take her after school if she didn't get detention, which she had miraculously managed to avoid. But after leaving the skatepark, as they walked up Main Street, Finley's stomach fluttered. She looked at Dale, walking calmly beside her.

"Aren't you nervous?"

"Nope."

"But what if we get caught? Will we get in trouble?"

Dale shrugged.

"I doubt it."

"What if someone sees and calls the police?"

Finley had talked to the police a few times when they came to her house looking for one of her mom's boyfriends. Sometimes, when she was still at the park near dusk, Officer

David offered her a ride home. He had a gap in between his two front teeth, smelled like root beer, and always gave her bubble gum.

"They won't."

Finley wasn't completely satisfied, but she stopped asking questions. When they got to the store the door was wide open, but Dale didn't go in right away.

"We have to make sure there's no one inside."

He craned his neck and peered into the entryway, listening. Determining the coast was clear, he looked up and down the street, grabbed Finley's hand, and swept them through the doorway. The stairs seemed steeper and narrower than they'd looked from outside, and Finley climbed them slowly. Something didn't feel quite right, but she kept quiet. The stairway opened into a large room with windows on three sides. There were two doors on the back wall and jewelry cases arranged in a big square in the middle of the room. By the time Finley reached the top of the stairs, Dale was shining his flashlight into the glass cases.

"What are you doing?"

He looked up and grinned sheepishly.

"Checking to see if they left anything."

"What's behind those doors?"

"The one on the left is a bathroom. The one on the right is locked."

Finley walked slowly around the room, looking into the dusty jewelry cases and sneaking glances out the window. Suddenly, she gasped.

"Dale, look!"

He looked up.

"What? What's the matter?"

She pointed and answered in a tiny voice.

"Our footprints."

Her trail of footprints had followed her through the thick dust covering the floor, and Dale's showed exactly where he'd wandered around the room, both last week and today. Dale laughed.

"Silly. Nobody ever comes up here. It's fine."

"But what if they do?"

He scrutinized her footprints, brushing his dirty blonde hair out of his eyes. His dad always prompted him to notice details and decipher their meaning.

"Our feet aren't that big. I don't think anyone would care that a couple kids came up here and looked around."

Finley looked thoughtfully at her tracks, then walked over to the back of the room. The bathroom door swung open easily, revealing a toilet, sink, and mirror on the far wall. The sink and toilet were both robin's egg blue.

"Ooooooo."

"What?"

Dale paused from his jewelry case search a second time as Finley waved him over.

"Isn't it pretty?"

Dale shrugged.

"If you like blue." He looked back at the jewelry cases. "I've almost looked through all of these. See if the bottom cabinets open."

Finley pulled on the cabinet handles. All were locked but the last one she tried, which was empty. As she was looking into it, they heard a pitchy female voice from the street below.

"I thought it would be a good idea to get here a little early and check on things."

A deep male voice answered,

"Me too. Last week I was driving past and saw a kid come out. Pluto probably left the door unlocked and it swung open—"

The woman interrupted.

"Just like it is today? For being so smart, he's very forgetful. Hopefully there's no one inside. That would be a pain."

Finley's eyes met Dale's above the jewelry case and she hissed,

"Get in here."

She crammed herself into the small cabinet, and Dale pushed in after her, pulling the door closed behind him. Swallowing their frantic breathing, they listened to the muffled footsteps come up the stairs. When they reached the top, the man grunted and the woman said,

"Well, whoever that boy was, he certainly wandered around up here. Look at all these footprints."

If Dale tilted his head at a certain angle, he could press one eye up against a crack in the cabinet door and see out. The cabinet creaked as the adults walked past, and Dale saw two sets of feet—one pair of brown men's loafers, and a pair of pink women's sneakers—walk past.

"There's nobody up here anymore," the man said. "He probably just saw the door open and wanted to look around. I bet he won't come back, but if he does, you know the plan."

"Yes, but our plan is for adults, not kids. The town will go crazy if a kid turns up missing."

Dale gasped. Finley kicked him. Missing? Who were these people, and what were they doing?

3

THE AIR IN THE small locked cabinet was stuffy. Finley needed to sneeze and Dale's leg was cramped and he had to pee, but they didn't dare move. They wondered what the creaks and thumps outside the cabinet were until Minnie said,

"If we weren't here first we wouldn't have to set up the chairs."

Her companion snorted.

"There are only five chairs, Minnie. Calm down. Besides, you're the one who wanted to get here early."

They sat down and talked about the weather and the local football team and the last "gig." A few minutes later, Dale and Finley heard muffled footsteps on the stairs.

"It's about time, Pluto," the woman said. "The meeting starts in five minutes and you're the first one here. You'd think nobody cares about punctuality anymore."

Mrs. O'Malley often lectured Finley about punctuality when Finley was running into the classroom at the last minute: "Miss Pike, punctuality is of the *utmost* importance in this class."

Once on her way to class, Finley helped a girl who dropped her books and papers in the hallway. When she hurried in a few minutes late, Mrs. O'Malley asked her if she would ever be on time. Finley hadn't bothered to answer, which got her an additional lecture.

Finley's mind snapped back to the present when she heard the voice of the newest arrival. It was deep and throaty, and Dale could see legs connected to muddy work boots in front of the cabinet.

"Minnie, the meeting doesn't start till I get here. I was checking out the scene of the crime. And besides, I wasn't the first one here. You two were."

The first man, Minnie's original companion, laughed, but Finley's palms went cold. Dale forgot that he had to pee.

Minnie's reply sounded injured.

"I was just joking. By the way, Mickey saw some boy coming out the door one day last week, and now there are a bunch of footprints in the dust. Looks like he was snooping around."

The owner of the newest voice spoke again.

"Probably just a curious kid. There's nothing for him to see up here anyways, and I'm sure he won't be back. If he does, he'll regret it."

Dale gulped at the man's sinister words.

"Now let's see. We're missing Daisy and Goofy. Anybody seen either of them today?"

The woman, who Dale and Finley would learn was always the first to answer, responded,

"You know I don't get groceries on Tuesdays, and even if I went to the city office, I wouldn't try to talk to Goofy."

The first man grunted in agreement, and the newcomer said,

"Well, I'll just use the bathroom before they get here."

They heard the bathroom door close and the woman, Minnie, say to her original companion,

"He's grumpy today."

The man mumbled. Almost since they'd arrived, the man's responses to her had been grunts or single-word statements. The children heard more footsteps on the stairs, and a moment later another pair of women's shoes stepped in front of his crack. A sing-song voice asked,

"Hello, everyone. I'm not late, right?"

Minnie was mid-response when the man came out of the bathroom and interrupted her.

"Don't listen to whatever Minnie says, you're not late. Did you see Goofy on your way here?"

A moment later, another set of footsteps sounded on the stairs and a man called up,

"Everybody here? Should I lock the door?"

Minnie, as usual, answered first.

"Yes!"

After Goofy came up the stairs and the group had a few minutes of small talk, the throaty-voiced man Minnie called Pluto said,

"We don't have all day, people. Let's get started."

Dale and Finley, cramped and both needing to pee by now, tried to pay attention to what the man was saying, but his voice was muffled and it was hard to concentrate in the stuffy cabinet. Finley rested her head on her knees and drifted off to sleep. Dale wiggled his toes one at a time to stay awake. The deep-voiced man was talking about a rich old dead guy who was buried with a sack of gold on each side of his head.

Dale remembered what he'd heard at church the week before, that you can't take money with you when you die. He felt sorry for the old guy. His ears perked up when Pluto, the man in charge, said,

"A week from Thursday is a new moon. So we have nine days to get ourselves in order. Does everyone remember what they're in charge of?"

Dale listened intently. He'd somehow missed the transition from the old man with the gold to an actual project. As his mind raced to remember what they'd said, Finley snored.

He urgently tapped her knee and listened, hoping that no one heard. Finley opened her eyes and could just make out Dale holding a finger over his lips in the dim cabinet. She rubbed her eyes.

Minnie answered Pluto's question first.

"I'm in charge of getting everybody new masks."

The other woman, Daisy, spoke next.

"I'm sharpening the shovels and making sure the lock-picking kit is in order, especially after what happened last time."

A murmur went around the group as Minnie retorted.

"If Mickey would have done a better job planning the diversion, we would've had more time."

The man who'd arrived first, Mickey, defended himself.

"It's not my fault the old lady slept with a gun by her pillow. The police barely even hurried to the call. They knew she could handle herself."

Pluto interrupted them.

"Stop acting like children. It doesn't matter what happened last time. Mickey, just make sure you do your homework on the diversion this time. Gas station, maybe? Or bank? We need a solid two hours. Goofy, plan to have transportation for at least ten people. I'm hoping for a few extra hands."

Goofy, the young man who'd arrived last, answered,

"I can manage that."

Pluto continued,

"I'll be sending the message out to the Cadillac, Traverse City, and Petoskey SODDs, to see how many additional hands we can get. I'll let you know if we need to meet again, otherwise, keep an eye out for the time and specific location for next Thursday night. I'll put it in the usual place."

Minnie broke in.

"Are you sure the usual place is still good? It just seems so . . . Obvious."

There were murmurs of agreement until Pluto asked,

"How many times have we done this?"

After a brief pause, Daisy answered.

"A lot. Maybe a hundred."

"Have we ever been caught?"

Moments of silence, followed by Minnie's reluctant,

"No."

"If it ain't broke, don't fix it. Look in the usual place."

They wrapped up a few more details, then Pluto said,

"If everything goes according to plan, this will be one of the biggest scores the Malvern SODD has taken since we started. This could set us all up nicely."

Minnie cackled and blurted,

"We could stop!" No one responded. Minnie continued, "Kidding, kidding. Of course we won't stop."

The folding chairs creaked as the group closed them. Then five pairs of feet clunked down the stairs, and the door below slammed. Dale sighed deeply in the silence, and Finley said,

"Quick, lemme out!"

But Dale didn't move.

"Not yet. We have to wait a while to make sure the coast is clear."

Finley groaned.

"How long is a while?"

Dale didn't answer right away. He wanted to get out as much as Finley did, but he knew it would be bad if anyone from the group saw them leave the building. His legs were tingling, his stomach hurt from needing to pee, and he knew it was getting dark. If he didn't hurry home, he would get in trouble for being late to dinner. Finley tapped her fingers against the side of the cabinet impatiently. After brief consideration, Dale said,

"Let's count to five hundred. They should be gone by then."

He counted slowly and precisely, not changing pace when Finley sped up or slowed down. When he reached 500, he eased the cabinet door open and listened. He heard a car pass, but no voices. Climbing out, he straightened and shook his legs to make them stop stinging. Then he peeked out the window. There were no cars or people, and even though it was dusk, the streetlights weren't on yet.

"Quick, Finley. The faster we go, the better."

She crawled out of the cabinet and whimpered,

"My legs hurt."

"Mine too. Let's go."

They hobbled down the stairs. When Dale decided the coast was clear, he pulled open the door and pushed Finley through it, following right behind her.

"Quick!"

He whispered as he took her hand and started running up the street. She limped behind him. After a few blocks he slowed to a walk. Finley spoke first.

"What are they going to dig up?"

"I'm not sure. They were talking about an old guy who was buried with sacks of gold."

They discussed everything they could remember from the conversation, but didn't come to any conclusion. When they got to Dale's house, Dale said,

"I should go inside. I don't want to be late for dinner."

Finley nodded and chewed her lip. Dale asked,

"What's the matter?"

Finley hesitated.

"That was scary." Dale shrugged. "Weren't you scared?"

He considered.

"Well, maybe a little. But not really."

"What? Why?"

She looked at him with incredulity.

"I was talking to Jesus."

Finley frowned.

"Who?"

"Jesus. You know, God?"

Shrugging, Finley said,

"We don't go to church."

"You don't have to go to church to talk to Jesus."

As the last word came out of his mouth, his mother opened the front door.

"Dale, it's time for dinner." Dale nodded and turned. His mother looked at Finley, who gazed hungrily after Dale. "Finley, would you like to eat with us?"

Finley nodded eagerly. As they walked up the steps into the house, Dale said,

"Let's not tell anybody about this for now, okay?"

It hadn't occurred to Finley to tell anyone. Steve didn't give her the time of day, and her mom wouldn't care.

"Okay."

When the whole family was seated around the table, Finley reached for her fork—but as she picked it up, Mr. Kellogg said,

"Let's pray."

Finley held her fork and looked around the table at the rest of the family, who sat with their heads bowed and eyes closed. She did neither, and continued to watch them as Mr. Kellogg cleared his throat and said,

"Dear Jesus, thank you for this food, thank you that we get to share dinner with Finley, and thank you for the beautiful fall colors. Please help us to bring you glory with the energy this food gives us. In your name we pray, amen."

When he finished, everyone opened their eyes and looked up. Finley loaded her fork and took a massive bite. They ate cheeseburger casserole, baked beans, and fresh veggies for dinner, and apple pie with ice cream for dessert. Finley even licked the ice cream off her plate. She never ate meals like that at her house. Her mom seldom cooked anything, and somehow even when she went shopping there still didn't seem to be much food. When dinner was over, Dale's mom asked,

"Would you like a ride home?"

Finley eagerly accepted. The car smelled like flowers and coconut, and the seats were smooth and squishy, not like the hard, torn seats in the minivan that Finley's mom drove. The house was dark when Dale's mom pulled into the driveway.

"Is someone home?"

"Steve. He never leaves."

Mrs. Kellogg asked who Steve was, and Finley told her. Then she went inside. Sure enough, Steve was watching TV. Finley stood by the door and asked,

"Where's mom?" He didn't show any signs of comprehension, so Finley asked again, louder. "Steve! Where's mom?"

Turning his head slowly, he looked at her and blinked.

"Dunno. Haven't seen 'er."

Finley sighed. She went to her room, closed the door, and went to bed. As she lay there, she kept hearing the voices from earlier echoing in her mind. Nothing she tried to distract herself with overwhelmed the sinister voice.

Yes, but the town will notice if a kid goes missing.

She hoped she never ran into those people again.

31

4

MRS. O'MALLEY HELD up an old orange book.

"Who knows what book this is?" No one raised a hand, so she continued, "This is our new book for reading hour. It's called *The Adventures of Tom Sawyer*."

Occasionally, Mrs. O'Malley read out loud to the class. Finley loved it. She felt like she became a part of the story when Mrs. O'Malley read. Today, she drew while she listened, but it didn't take long for her to forget the pencil in her hand and stare into space, spellbound. She felt a kinship to Tom Sawyer, because he was always in trouble. She was always in trouble too. At lunch, Dale told her he had a hard time falling asleep the night before.

"Me too. I wish we could just forget about them."

"Let's not go past the jewelry store today."

They munched quietly on their nachos—one of the best lunches the school served—while sitting at a table off to the side of the cafeteria so Dale could watch everything that was going on. Today, a new boy sat alone a few tables away. Only his toes touched the ground, but he swung his legs peacefully back and forth. His big brown glasses kept sliding down his nose as he munched happily on crackers and read a book. An apple and two pre-packaged chocolate cupcakes were on the table next to him.

Finley looked at him curiously. He reminded her a little bit of Dale. She gestured over at him and asked,

"He's new, right? Do you have any classes with him?"

Dale nodded.

"Just one. He doesn't say much. His name is Dean."

Finley studied Dean as Rusty sauntered over to his table. Dean ate his crackers in oblivion, and Rusty leaned over him. In the busy cafeteria, it was hard to hear what he said, but Finley could guess. Rusty fingered the cupcakes and edged them closer to himself. Dean, holding a hand in the book, looked up at Rusty and shook his head, but Rusty just smirked and tightened his grip on the cellophane. Finley watched in growing frustration.

The package was at the edge of the table now. Suddenly, Dean realized what was happening. He swiped for the cupcakes, but Rusty snapped them up, holding his hand in the air high above Dean's jumps.

Before Finley knew what she was doing, she'd slipped off her bench and approached the two boys. Rusty was taunting Dean.

"What's the matter, little one, can't reach your sweets?"

Dean tried to grab the cupcakes, but he was way too short. When Finley reached him, she stood on her tiptoes and stuck her face right up to Rusty, ignoring the nacho crumbs and cheese around his mouth.

"Give him his cupcakes, Rusty."

He considered her and then shook his head.

"What if I don't?"

"Then I'll tell Mr. Munson I saw you cheating on the English test last week."

Rusty scowled but didn't lower his hand. While Finley was talking, Dale crept around behind Rusty and climbed up on the bench. Right as Rusty was launching into another taunt, Dale plucked the cupcakes easily from his hand. Rusty spun around, but Dale had already jumped down and backed away. He said,

"Leave him alone, Rusty."

Rusty looked between the three of them and decided it would be too much work for two small cupcakes. He shrugged and said,

"Whatever. They look nasty anyway."

His retreating swagger was a little less cocky. Dean said,

"Thanks, guys."

They nodded and introduced themselves, then invited Dean to sit at their table. His family had just moved from California, and Finley and Dale peppered him with questions about what it was like there. It helped them avoid talking about the jewelry store.

They didn't go near it after school either. They hung out on the middle school playground and ate dinner at Dale's house every night for the rest of the week. Now Finley expected the pre-dinner prayer. After her third dinner at

Dale's house, while they were playing a board game, she asked him about it.

"Why do you guys do that?"

Dale was confused.

"What?"

"Pray before you eat?"

"Jesus gives us everything, even the food we eat. We want to thank Him."

His simple answer seemed to satisfy her, and she mumbled,

"Jesus. Hmm."

He tilted his head and looked at her, but didn't say anything else.

On Friday night in the car in Finley's driveway, Dale's mother invited Finley to a corn maze. Finley eagerly accepted the invitation. She'd never been to a corn maze.

On the ride there the next day, Dale taught Finley a car trip game where they had to find the alphabet on license plates. When they arrived, Dale's parents told them to be back for lunch in two hours. Dale and Finley took off running toward the giant ear of corn that marked the maze entrance. Someone dressed as a corn cob handed them a map, which Dale shoved into his pocket as they entered the maze.

After coming to multiple dead ends, they emerged into a wide open area with a bench and a big sign shaped like a pumpkin. Painted onto the pumpkin were the words, "You made it!"

Finley said,

"That wasn't very hard."

Dale shook his head.

"It usually isn't." He pulled the wrinkled map out of his pocket and continued, "Let's explore."

They wandered around the maze, playing tag and hiding in the corn to watch people pass. Finley wanted to jump out and scare them, but Dale wouldn't let her. They were watching a family with two small children when Dale looked at his watch.

"It's time for lunch!"

They pushed out of the corn and ran toward what Dale thought was the entrance—only to find a dead end. They tried another path. It was another dead end. Finley was hungry and tired.

"I thought you knew where we were."

Dale wasn't put off by her grumpy tone.

"I thought so too. Sorry. Let's try another way."

After a half-dozen more dead ends, they finally came to a wide twisting path. Dale, who had been studying his map, said,

"This should be the way out."

They followed the path to the outside of the maze—but when they came out, both looked around in confusion. They weren't in the pumpkin patch and the giant ear of corn was nowhere to be seen. Instead, they were standing behind a big red barn. Finley groaned.

"You said this was the way out!"

Dale studied the wrinkled map in his sweaty palm and said,

"I thought it was!"

"It was all right, out to somebody's house!"

Finley's hunger was turning to crankiness. She sat down in frustration. Dale frowned at the map.

"I don't think that path is even on here."

Finley didn't care what was or wasn't on the map. She just didn't want to miss lunch.

"I'm hungry. What if there's no food left by the time we get back?"

Dale was studying the map and didn't reply. Neither one noticed the tall, burly man walking toward them. When he spoke, both flinched.

"Are you kids lost?"

Finley froze. She instantly recognized the deep, throaty voice with its hint of gruff impatience. As soon as he spoke, Finley jumped up, reached for Dale's elbow, and apologized.

"We're sorry mister. We were trying to get out of the corn maze and we followed a path and it came out here. I'm not sure what happened." She tugged at Dale's arm. His eyes seemed to be frozen on his map, but they were actually fixed on the man's muddy work boots.

The man grunted.

"You must have gotten pretty lost. The pumpkin patch is all the way on the other end of this field. If you go straight into the field and follow a row of corn, you'll get there eventually. But it'll take a while."

Both children nodded.

"We're really sorry about that," Finley said. Then, in an urgent undertone, "Dale, *let's go.*"

Dale looked at the man's face. His wide eyebrows, big nose, and thin lips somehow matched his throaty voice. As they turned back toward the corn field, Dale said,

"Thanks for your help." They walked until Dale felt like they were out of sight, then he whispered, "Let's run."

Finley followed him down the row of corn. The leaves whipped her face, arms, and hair, but she didn't care. They ran until Finley's breath was burning in her throat and her chest hurt and she had a cramp in her side, but Dale wouldn't stop. Instead, he kept urging her to run faster. Finley put one foot in front of the other until she couldn't go any more. Heaving one last panting breath, she yelped,

"Dale!" Then she stopped running, took a deep breath, and gasped, "I . . . can't . . ."

Dale, just as winded, slowed to a walk. The maze seemed so much bigger than it had when they first entered it a few hours ago. When Finley caught her breath enough to talk, she said,

"Dale. It was the guy. It was Pluto."

Dale nodded.

"I know."

"We saw him. *He saw us.* What are we going to do?"

Dale shook his head.

"He doesn't know about us, silly. We don't have to do anything."

They walked on in silence. After what seemed like forever, they emerged right next to the pumpkin patch. Dale's family was sitting at a picnic table near the gigantic red barn. Dale's dad said,

"We were getting ready to send a search party."

"Sorry we're late. We got lost and came out on the other side of the field in some guy's yard."

Dale's dad raised his eyebrows, and Finley asked,

"Is there any food left for us?"

A sad look flew across Mrs. Kellogg's face as she answered.

"Of course! We waited for you—well, Patty didn't. She couldn't wait."

Patty, eager to be the center of attention, waved her crumby hands around to show Finley the soggy cracker she was clutching.

Mrs. Kellogg pulled containers out of the picnic basket, and Finley's mouth started watering. There was potato salad, coleslaw, fruit salad, veggies, chips and salsa, chicken salad sandwiches, and chocolate cake. Finley quickly sat down and folded her hands in her lap. After a week of eating with Dale's family, she was getting into the habit of praying before meals, even if she didn't completely understand it.

Mr. Kellogg thanked God for the lunch, then Mrs. Kellogg handed Finley a paper plate heaped high with food. She barely remembered to say thank you before picking up a fork and digging into the potato salad.

When she finished eating, Finley was so stuffed she could barely move. She flopped down on a picnic blanket with Dale and they looked at the white puffy clouds, pointing out shapes to each other.

In the car on their way home, Dale and Finley whispered about seeing Pluto. Finley asked,

"Do you think it was his house?"

Dale nodded.

"I guess it's good we know where he lives, just in case we need to find him."

Finley frowned. She couldn't imagine wanting to find Pluto—she wanted nothing to do with him. But the thought that those people were going to do something on Thursday kept coming back to her. She didn't know what it was, but she had the nagging feeling it was bad.

Who was Pluto, really? Was he actually dangerous? A chill ran down her spine at her next thought: Even though he didn't know who they were, now he knew what they looked like.

5

ON MONDAY MORNING, Mr. Slinch told Finley to sit down three times in a row. The first time she pretended not to hear him. The second time she told him she didn't want to. And the third time, because she already knew she would go to detention, she stuck her tongue out and rolled her eyes back into her head, moaning like a ghost.

Mr. Slinch sighed, wrote her a detention slip, and thought about the vacation he had booked for the Bahamas in the middle of December. It couldn't come soon enough.

In Mrs. O'Malley's class, Rusty Cowell was back to his old tricks. He'd been good for a few days after tripping her, and the incident in the cafeteria, but when he went unpunished, he took it as a free pass to continue tormenting her. As Finley hurried into class at the last moment, he smirked. She frowned and slid into her seat—only to yelp and jump up. There was a tack on her chair. She picked it up and threw it at Rusty, who sneered in satisfaction. Mrs. O'Malley turned around and raised an eyebrow, so Finley sat down, took a deep breath, and reached for her notebook and pencil. As she bent her head to rummage in her backpack, a wet glob of paper hit her neck. Rusty snickered. Finley shook her head, determined to dissolve the overpowering red mist in front of her eyes.

She concentrated on the lines in her notebook. For a moment, it seemed like she would be able to handle her anger—but Rusty wasn't done. While Mrs. O'Malley was writing on the board, Rusty eased his chunky frame from his chair and edged over to Finley's desk. When his hot breath hit her neck she flinched. He whispered,

"My mom says your mom is a welfare queen who sleeps around." He lowered his voice even more and continued, "She calls her a *slut*."

That was enough. Finley didn't attempt to control her rage—she didn't want to. Leaping from her chair, she hammered her fists into Rusty's stomach, screaming,

"Rusty Cowell, you're a BULLY and a COWARD, and my mom's not a slut—YOUR MOM IS!"

Rusty immediately crumpled in agony. Mrs. O'Malley's usually gentle voice thundered from the whiteboard as she glared at them from behind the rims of her thick wire-frame glasses.

"RUSTY, FINLEY, COME WITH ME."

There would be no argument and no stalling. Finley meekly followed Mrs. O'Malley down the hall, and Rusty shuffled along whimpering. They walked past Mitchell Fitzwell as he dusted the tops of lockers. He watched the procession—pitiful Finley, unrepentant Rusty, and irate Mrs.

O'Malley—proceed down the hallway. Shaking his head, he kept dusting.

As they passed, Finley wondered if he really was a magician, and if so, if he would cast a spell on her that would make her disappear for the rest of the day. Maybe the rest of the year.

Mrs. O'Malley marched both students straight into the principal's office where Mr. Munson, reading something on his computer and tapping his knuckles on the desk, looked up at them. He was a calm, kind principal who often walked the halls and looked in on classes. The skin around his eyes crinkled when he smiled. Students, even the ones who were frequently in trouble, like Finley, didn't mind him. They knew he cared about them.

Standing there breathing fury, Mrs. O'Malley spluttered,

"There was an . . . an *altercation* in my class, Mr. Munson. I didn't see the whole thing, but . . . but I believe *she* is the perpetrator."

She pointed accusingly at Finley, who stared down at her toes. Mr. Munson looked at the trio.

"Thank you, Mrs. O'Malley. I'll take it from here."

Mrs. O'Malley marched out, bringing her frustration with her. Mr. Munson looked at the children in silence. Finley was still studying her shoes, and Rusty was bent almost double, holding his stomach. Mr. Munson invited them both to sit.

Finley liked Mr. Munson's office. He kept a row of desk toys on the edge of his desk, and he usually let her play with them for a few minutes before sending her back to class. But today she didn't even look at them. She slumped back in her seat and focused on the scuffed knees of her pants. Mr. Munson looked at Rusty.

"Mister Cowell, would you like to tell me what happened?"

Rusty whined,

"I was minding my own business and she stood up and whopped me in the stomach and said rude things about my mom!"

Mr. Munson raised an eyebrow, and the red anger cascaded through Finley's mind again at hearing his explanation. She took a deep breath as Mr. Munson asked,

"Is that everything?"

Rusty nodded self-righteously. Mr. Munson looked at Finley and asked,

"Miss Pike, is this true?"

For a split second, Finley was quiet. Her answer could make a lifetime enemy out of Rusty, which could be terrible—but he was already the closest thing she had to a lifetime enemy, and she didn't really care. She shook her head vehemently.

"No. I got to class and there was a tack on my chair. Then he hit me with a spitball, then he came over and whispered in my ear that my mom is a—" here, Finley stopped short. The words were not pleasant to repeat. Even though she would never admit it, Finley knew deep down that they held some truth.

Mr. Munson prompted her.

"Go on."

She took a deep breath and blurted,

"That my mom is awelfarequeenwhosleepsaround." She winced, then continued, "And he called her a *slut*. Then I punched him."

It wasn't smug. It was just matter-of-fact, like she was saying what she ate for breakfast. Mr. Munson knew that it was wrong for Rusty to say what he'd said, but he knew there was some truth in it. He also knew that Rusty's life wasn't very easy either. His father was a workaholic bully and his mother spent most of their money on cigarettes and lottery tickets.

Rusty spluttered,

"That's not true!"

But his words lacked conviction, and Finley looked pleadingly at Mr. Munson, who said,

"Shall I call one of your classmates down to ask them what happened?"

Finley answered,

"Sure. Go ahead."

But Rusty shook his head, knowing he was outsmarted. Mr. Munson said,

"Huh. That's what I thought. What do you recommend your punishment should be?"

Mr. Munson often asked students this question. If the answer was reasonable, he usually incorporated it into their consequence. Finley usually asked to sit quietly in his office for the rest of the class period. It barely felt like a consequence. But she knew that today Mrs. O'Malley was reading about Tom Sawyer and she didn't want to miss it.

"Mrs. O'Malley is reading out loud in class and I really want to hear it. I already have detention today from Mr.

Slinch. Can I just have it again tomorrow and go back to class right now?"

Mr. Munson nodded.

"Yes, detention for both of you tomorrow will be fine, but I expect better from both of you in the future." He looked evenly at them. Finley nodded and looked at her feet, but Rusty didn't make eye contact. "Finley, you may go back to class. Rusty, a word?"

Finley stood. All things considered, it had turned out better than she'd expected.

"Thank you, Mr. Munson."

He nodded, and she hurried out. As she left the office, she heard him begin, "Now, Rusty, do you . . ." but she didn't stick around to hear what he said.

Back in the classroom, she slipped into her seat and listened attentively as Mrs. O'Malley read. Tom and his friends were playing Robin Hood in the woods. When Mrs. O'Malley reached the end of the chapter, she paused.

"Shall I read the next chapter?"

A chorus of "Yes!" rose up from around the room, and she smiled.

The chapter opened with Tom in bed waiting. When it was almost midnight, he snuck out of the house and went to the graveyard with Huckleberry Finn. They brought a dead cat to perform a wart removal spell, but before they could complete it they saw three figures that looked like ghosts.

Finley sat on the edge of her seat, entranced. When the ghosts turned out to be three people, she sighed in relief. But then they began to dig up a grave—and suddenly a bell went off in Finley's mind. Her mouth dropped open, and she turned to look at Dale. He was staring at her, wide eyed. Scribbling a note, he passed it to her.

They're GRAVE ROBBERS.

Finley scrawled back,

What do we do?

Mrs. O'Malley chose that moment to look up and see Dale reading the note. She said,

"Mister Kellogg, feel free to continue your conversation after class, please."

Dale sheepishly stuffed the slip of paper into his pocket. Finley tried to pay attention to the rest of the chapter—which included a grim murder and the two terrified boys, the only witnesses, running away in terror—but she kept thinking back to the conversation from the jewelry store. It all made sense now! They were going to dig up the gold that was buried with the rich dead man. What if she and Dale were the only ones who knew and the only ones who could stop them?

The rest of the afternoon dragged by and when the final bell rang, Dale followed Finley to her locker.

"I can't believe I didn't think of that before."

Finley was digging through her locker, looking for an extra notebook. She grunted.

"I mean, I guess robbing graves isn't a super common crime."

Dale shrugged.

"But still, I should have thought of it." He shuffled his feet, waiting for some reassurance, but Finley didn't answer. "Anyway, come over to my house after detention and we'll figure out what to do."

Detention dragged by. Finley did her homework then gazed longingly out the window. The leaves were beginning to change colors, the sky was blue, and the sun was shining. After what felt like years, the teacher released them. Finley rushed out, ran down the empty halls, and burst through the front doors. She didn't bother to go home and drop her backpack off, instead she ran all the way to Dale's house. He was sitting on the front porch playing with Patty. When he saw her, he said,

"That seemed longer than usual."

"It felt like forever."

She threw her backpack onto the deck and plopped down next to it. Gesturing at a plate of cookies, Dale asked,

"Want a cookie?" While Finley munched, Dale said, "It's so simple that I can't believe we didn't see it. Everything makes sense now. I feel dumb."

The shovels, the diversion, the masks, digging during a new moon, it all fell into place. Dale wanted to tell the police right away, but when he suggested it, Finley said,

"But we have no idea where or what time they'll be digging, besides that it's on Thursday. If we don't know anything else, they might not believe us."

There were two graveyards in town—the currently used graveyard right outside of town that was well-kept and neatly manicured, and one a few miles out that was overgrown and abandoned. Dale nodded.

"I guess you're right. We have to look for more clues." Finley dreaded what she knew he would say next. "I think we need to go back to the jewelry store."

"Are you sure?"

"Do you have a better idea?"

Finley shook her head. Dale jumped up and sent Patty inside, yelling to his mom that they were leaving. Standing reluctantly, Finley said,

"You sound excited."

He shrugged.

"A little, I guess. I feel like a detective."

But the door to the jewelry store was closed and locked. Relief washed over Finley.

"Looks like we can't go in."

They looked up at the windows, then sat on the curb in front of the store. Dale was trying to remember if Pluto said anything about how he would contact the team. Finley looked at her toes and watched an ant scurry around. For how productive everyone said ants were, they certainly wandered a lot. Dale interrupted her thoughts.

"Remember when they were talking about putting the message in the usual place?" Finley nodded. "And how Minnie didn't think it was a good idea because of how obvious the usual place is?" Finley nodded again. "If it's that obvious, don't you think we could find it?"

Finley nodded a third time.

"But what's that obvious?"

Dale narrowed his eyes and studied the antique store across the street. A sign out front read, *Sale this weekend, Friday–Sunday! 50% off all items from after 1901.*

"What if it's on a sign?"

Finley snorted.

"That would be crazy. They're not just going to put the time and place of the robbery on a sign for everyone to see."

"Well, maybe that's why Minnie hated the idea. Maybe it's on a sign in code."

Shrugging, Finley said,

"I guess it's our best idea so far."

"Let's make a list of all the signs in town."

Malvern, population 1,900, is a small town on an east to west highway that runs across central Michigan. There's one stoplight where Main Street crosses the highway, and a blinking yellow light on the road that the high school is on.

Main Street is lined with shops on both sides of the street—there are quilting and craft shops, offices, antique shops, a smoke shop, a dance studio, and a clothing boutique—but none of them have signs besides the company names above the door. The changeable signs are all on the strip of highway that runs through the town, where there are a few restaurants, two gas stations, a small family-run grocery store called Fosty's, a coffee shop that locals call Drippy's, and a handful of other businesses.

"Well, the big gas station has one. And McDonalds. And Fosty's." Dale scribbled down the names, and Finley squeezed her eyes closed, thinking hard.

"Doesn't Drippy's have a sign?" Dale nodded, adding it to his list, and Finley continued. "And Smith Lumber?" Dale kept scribbling while Finley came up with a half-dozen more signs. When they couldn't think of anywhere else, Dale jumped up.

"We'd better hurry."

Finley stood and they ran down Main Street toward the stoplight. Once there, they turned onto the large highway sidewalk. The first sign they saw was for one of the two gas stations. It read, *Hot coffee, 50 cents a cup.*

Dale shook his head.

"That's not it.

The next business with a sign was the Lighthouse Cafe. It had a light-up LED sign that flashed different phrases. They stood and watched the entire cycle of phrases, which included, *Come in for lunch, Breakfast at 6:30*, and *Try our bacon burger.*

"That sign makes me hungry," Finley commented.

"You're always hungry."

She shrugged in acknowledgment as they moved on down the street, reading every sign. None seemed to say anything about a time or place. When they passed McDonald's, Finley stopped.

"It's not here. Let's go to the park and think of something else."

But Dale said,

"We still have one sign left." He pointed at the Fosty's Grocery sign. "We just have to get a little closer."

When they were close enough, Finley read the sign out loud.

"Eggs: 80 cents per dozen. Milk: 1.99 per gallon. Cereal: Buy one, get one free." She paused. "Seems normal to me."

Dale copied down the words, like he'd done for every other sign they saw, then studied his piece of paper in disappointment.

"I really thought that would be it."

"I'm sure there's something else obvious," Finley said. They sat on the swings and tried to think of other ways a criminal would communicate with his team.

"I just don't know what's more obvious than a sign on the side of the road." Dean scratched his head as he talked, then stopped abruptly and said, "The newspaper?"

"It can't be the newspaper because that doesn't come out often enough," Finley said.

Finley's mom didn't get the newspaper, but she knew from their neighbor, a middle-aged man named Mr. Arthwell, that it only came once a week. He was always complaining that current events were history by the time the newspaper came out. Finley suggested,

"Maybe the message just isn't up yet."

Dale looked at his paper and shrugged.

"I think we still need to go to the police. Even if we don't know when or where it is, this information is better than nothing."

Finley stood and started walking away. Dale called to her.

"Where are you going?"

"Didn't you want to tell the police?"

"Right now?"

"When else would we go?"

As they walked, Finley asked the question they were both considering.

"What are we going to say?"

Dale hesitated, then answered,

"I guess we'll tell them everything."

Finley nodded. When they got to the police station, Dale hesitated.

"What's the matter?"

He looked sheepish.

"I've never been in a police station before."

Finley grinned.

"It's not bad. If Mrs. Toller is there, she'll give us candy."

As they stepped inside, a wrinkled, gray-haired woman behind a glass window greeted them.

"How can I help you, Finley? Who's your friend?"

Motioning at Dale, Finley answered,

"Hi Mrs. Toller, this is Dale. We need to report a possible robbery. Is David here?"

Mrs. Toller looked at them seriously.

"Sounds important. David just stopped in. I'll get him." Before leaving the desk, she motioned toward the two chairs in the waiting area, saying, "Take a seat over there." Then she leaned forward and dropped two lollipops into the small indent in the counter, normally used for passing IDs. "You can eat these while you wait."

Dale took his lollipop and looked around. The walls were a light seafoam green, and there were posters on the walls about the dangers of drunk driving and doing drugs. The carpet on the floor was a threadbare tan. The chairs were stiff, but not uncomfortable. Finley hummed and licked her lollipop, blissfully unconcerned that it was turning her lips and tongue purple. Dale said,

"It's not that bad here."

Finley grinned.

"Did you think it would be?" He shrugged, and Finley said, "They're always nice to me. I like it."

Finley was done with her lollipop and Dale's was just a tiny nub on the end of the stick when a tall, broad man with thinning dark hair came out of the door near Mrs. Toller's window. He grinned, revealing a small gap in his front teeth.

"Hi, Miss Finley. I understand you're here on official business?"

Finley nodded.

"We're here to report a possible robbery. This is Dale."

David shook Dale's hand and said,

"Come back to my desk and I'll take down your comments." The wide metal door swung closed behind them with a loud *thud*. Dale stopped walking and looked around. Several desks were set in a grid pattern. Bulletin boards lined the walls. On one was a detailed street map of the town, on another was a topographical map of the township. There was even a board labeled, "Persons of Interest" with photos of people on it, and through the window in a door on the far side of the room, Dale saw cell bars.

Finley called, "Dale, come on!" then told David, "He's never been in a police station before."

David grinned.

"I see that." Dale was at David's desk now. "What's this about a robbery?"

The children looked at each other, and Finley nodded to Dale. Dale sheepishly told about the first time that he'd wandered through the open door of the abandoned jewelry store, then how he returned with Finley and they hid in the empty case when the other people appeared. David grinned, but the grin faded when Dale launched into a description of the meeting. When Dale paused after telling how they ran out of the jewelry store, David asked,

"So that's it?"

Finley shook her head violently.

"No. That was Tuesday. Saturday we went to the corn maze."

Finley described getting lost and coming out in Pluto's yard, then she launched into an explanation of why they hadn't come to the police sooner, because it wasn't until Mrs. O'Malley read *The Adventures of Tom Sawyer* that they realized maybe it was going to be a grave robbery. And they didn't know a time or place and they didn't want the police to doubt them because they were missing important details.

When she finished, Finley looked expectantly at David. He raised an eyebrow.

"You figured out it was a grave robbery from reading Tom Sawyer?" Both children nodded. "But you don't know when or where?"

They shook their heads.

"Well. Thank you for the tip. We'll keep our eyes open on Thursday night."

Finley and Dale exchanged a glance, then Finley asked, "That's it?"

"Is that all the information you have?" Finley nodded, and David continued, "Then I guess so. If you're right about this, it could be serious. I want the two of you to stay out of this. You could be in danger." Finley and Dale nodded, then David smiled. "Good. Want a ride home?"

Dale's eyes bugged out of his head when David opened the door of his squad car for them. David laughed.

"It's fine, you're not under arrest. I promise."

He winked at Finley. A few minutes later they pulled up in front of Dale's house. Dale's mom was reading with Patty on the front porch and when the squad car stopped in front of her house, she stood, frowning. David got out of the car and opened the back door for Finley and Dale. Mrs. Kellogg asked,

"Is everything okay, officer?"

David grinned. He'd often seen the Kellogg family sitting on the front porch or playing in the yard. He liked them.

"Yes ma'am, I was just giving them a ride home."

"They're not in trouble?"

"Of course not! They were reporting the grave robbery."

When David said "robbery," guilt crossed Dale's face. Mrs. Kellogg arched her eyebrows.

"Robbery?"

David looked between the trio, then said,

"It's quite the story."

Finley frowned.

"It's not just a story."

David nodded as he got back in his car. Mrs. Kellogg looked at Finley and Dale, who were both shuffling their feet.

"Something you need to tell me?"

Dale nodded. They sat on the porch and told her everything. Mrs. Kellogg listened intently. When they finished, she asked,

"When were you planning to tell us?"

Dale said,

"We didn't realize it was going to be a robbery until today in school. I guess I planned to tell you tonight."

"I see."

"Sorry, mom."

Mrs. Kellogg pulled him into a hug.

"I'm just glad the two of you are okay. You should always tell us if you feel like you're in danger. But you were trespassing in the jewelry store, and that's wrong. We'll have to see what your father says." Dale stepped back from his mother and grinned at Finley. But his grin faded as his mother said, "I do know, even without talking to him, that you can't have anything to do with this anymore. It's too risky. I don't want you to get hurt."

Finley frowned. But what if they were the only ones who could stop the robbery? How could they just give up?

WHEN FINLEY SAW Dale in the hall on Tuesday morning, he didn't flash his usual grin.

"What's the matter?"

He told Finley his dad grounded him for a week and said he wasn't allowed to have anything else to do with the robbery.

"He said he really didn't want me to get hurt, but they also want me to think more before I do stuff."

The bell rang and Finley hurried to class. Something about the finality of Dale's tone bothered her. Stopping the robbers was up to her now.

Finley sat quietly all through Mr. Slinch's science class, and at lunch, when she just picked at the macaroni and cheese, Dale said,

"Isn't this your favorite food? Why aren't you eating?'"

Finley mumbled back to him.

"Not hungry."

He frowned.

"Come on, Finley. You're always hungry." She sighed, and he added, "Besides, you sat still for Mr. Slinch. You never sit still in science class."

Then her words came flooding out.

"Dale, if we don't try to figure it out, who will? What if there's more to it than just a one-time robbery? What if stopping them is up to us?" He reminded her that they had told the police, but she frowned. "It didn't seem like David took us seriously."

"I think he did." In a desperate tone, he added, "Finley, please forget about it. If I have anything else to do with it, I'll get in way more trouble with my parents."

She shrugged, unmoved.

"I'm still going to try to figure it out alone. I'll be okay. I'm just a kid. No one will hurt me."

"But remember what they said about making kids disappear?"

Neither of them noticed Mitchell Fitzwell wheeling the trash cart behind them. When he heard their words, he stopped in his tracks. After a moment he moved on—but his face was puzzled. As Mitchell walked away, Dean came over to their table.

"Hey guys." Dale smiled and said hi, but Finley only tipped up her chin in acknowledgment. Dean sat down and continued, "I'm having a birthday party on Saturday. Will you guys come? I'm going to invite everyone in my class."

Dale nodded.

"I'd love to, but I'm grounded. I'll ask my parents."

Dean looked at Finley, who was still picking at her pasta. He asked,

"Finley?"

She nodded absentmindedly.

"Yeah, I'll come."

Dean ate in silence for a few minutes, then looked back and forth between the two of them.

"Is everything okay?"

Dale shrugged, but Finley said,

"We're trying to solve a mystery and I don't think the police believe us and now he's grounded because of the whole thing."

"Oh."

As she finished speaking the bell rang. They gathered their trays and left the cafeteria, parting ways in the hallway.

That afternoon when the detention teacher released the students, Finley didn't stand up to go. She was too distracted. Mrs. Meyer came over.

"Is everything okay, Finley?"

Finley jumped.

"What?"

Mrs. Meyer rolled her eyes.

"You can go. Detention is over."

Finley swept her incomplete homework into her backpack and bolted. She had to remind herself not to go straight to Dale's house from school. He wouldn't be able to do anything today.

When she stepped into her mom's house, Steve was snoring on the couch in the living room. She quietly dropped her backpack by the door and tiptoed into the kitchen. He probably wouldn't wake up, but Finley didn't want to take that chance.

The night before when she got home, he'd been fighting with her mom. Finley had gone straight to her room, but she could easily hear their yelling. When it finally died down, Steve stormed out and her mother sat at the kitchen table crying. Finley went into the kitchen to see her, and she pulled Finley into a tight hug.

"Maybe it'll just be us girls now. How do you like that?"

Finley had nodded. Her mother had no idea how much she would like that.

But Steve was back. Finley's disappointment momentarily distracted her from the robbery, but it did not distract her from her hunger. Her mom had finally gone shopping yesterday, so Finley poured herself a bowl of marshmallow charm cereal and munched quietly, thinking about what she could do to catch the robbers.

The rhythm of Steve's snoring broke, and Finley froze. She heard a grunt, then the snoring continued. Quietly slurping down the last of her milk and cereal, Finley put her bowl in the sink and slipped out the back door. Even though it might be worthless, she would check the signs again.

But a quick run through town revealed all the same words on every sign. Discouraged, she turned onto Main Street and sat on a bench in front of the library. It was tucked into the entrance nook across from a wall with a quote on it:

Books are the legacies that
a great genius leaves to mankind.
—Joseph Addison

The words were chiseled into the cement wall, and even though they'd faded over the years, they were still clear enough to read. She stared at them mindlessly. They reminded her of something, but she wasn't sure what. She watched cars pass and smiled at a few people coming out of the library, and when she looked back at the wall, she suddenly knew: A gravestone!

Suddenly Finley had an idea. What if the obvious clue, the hint that everyone could see but no one would notice, was at the cemetery?

She jumped up and ran to the walking path that went along the highway, following it to where it crossed the cemetery road. When she arrived at the graveyard, she plopped down on a bench at the outskirts to catch her breath.

The hill, dotted with trees, was covered in grave markers of various shapes and sizes. When she was no longer panting, Finley started walking through the stones. After going up and down more than a dozen rows, she leaned against one of the bigger stones and sighed. There didn't seem to be anything out of the ordinary. Maybe her idea was wrong.

Meanwhile, in a truck parked on the crest of a neighboring hill, a burly man with wide eyebrows, a big nose, and thin lips watched her impatiently. It was Pluto. He peered through his binoculars, muttering,

"Dumb kid. What's she doing here? I don't have all day."

In the bed of his pickup truck was an ornate wreath studded with yellow and white flowers. On the bottom loop of the wreath, two gaudy beaded numerals spelled 11. Pluto stopped watching the girl for long enough to look at his map of the cemetery. One name was circled with a red pen: Marv Jacobsen. Pluto's face broke into a greedy smile.

Marv died when Pluto was a young boy. He remembered the funeral—everyone in town went. The Jacobsens were a Malvern founding family. The funeral service was open casket, but the casket was closed on the drive between the church and the cemetery. Presumably that's when Marv's widow, Madge, deposited two large sacks of gold into the casket, one on either side of Marv's head.

Of course, Pluto hadn't seen the gold. Only Madge and the hearse driver knew for sure, and neither of them said anything about it for years. But a few weeks ago the hearse driver's son, now a grown man, had a few too many drinks at Reilly's Pub. Pluto was sitting nearby and heard him.

"My father had all kinds of secrets—it may be true that dead men tell no tales, but their families definitely do. On his deathbed, my father told me secrets about dozens of Malvern families that he'd kept for years. One of the best was about old Marv Jacobsen."

He'd gone on to tell, in drunken detail, of the two bags of gold and how Madge hadn't shed a single tear as she placed them beside Marv's head. Raising the pitch of his voice to mimic hers, he said,

"I always knew you loved your money more than you loved me. And look at you now, with no money. You left it for me, but I don't want it."

Pluto asked around after hearing the story. No one else seemed to know about the gold, which was good. Widespread rumors are seldom true, and if people knew about it, perhaps it already would have been stolen. But that wasn't good enough evidence to make him gather the team for a dig, so one afternoon he called the local bank and asked to speak with Kate Schmidt, the late hearse driver's daughter. She was a banker, and a slightly more dependable source than her drunken brother. Pluto pretended to be an old friend of her father's and ignored her polite attempts to get off the phone. After amusing himself by making up several stories about his adventures with her father, he lowered his voice.

"But do you know what he told me one time?" Kate was silent, so he continued. "He told me that he saw Madge Jacobsen put two bags of gold into the casket with Marv. Told me nobody knew, and that he'd take the secret to his grave."

The long pause on the other end of the line told Pluto he must be right. She finally said,

"Well, dad told lots of stories, and he wasn't all there when he got older."

Her voice was shaky.

"That happens to us old guys, I guess." Pluto laughed loudly, then said, "Well, thanks for the conversation. It was just like talking to your dad again."

As soon as he got off the phone, he called the meeting of the SODD that Finley and Dale accidentally attended in the jewelry shop. Now, a week later and two days before the dig, he was at the cemetery to leave the time and place marker— but that girl was wandering around between the headstones.

"Little pest," he mumbled, looking anxiously at his watch. He had a meeting at city hall in twenty minutes, and he did not want to be late. When she stopped and sat on a gravestone, he groaned. After a few more minutes, he started his truck and muttered,

"She's just a kid. She won't think anything of it."

He drove up to the graveyard, turned onto the long winding drive, and slowly pulled along it until he was close to Marv's grave. The girl was wandering between the headstones again, but on the far side at the top of the hill. Pluto left the truck running as he brought the wreath up to Marv's gravestone and propped it up against the marker. He pretended to take a moment of silence, then returned to his truck.

As he pulled out of the cemetery, he reached for his phone and dialed a number.

"Hey, Daisy? Sign is out." He paused, then replied, "Yep. Went off without a hitch."

He chuckled as he drove off. In a little more than 48 hours, he would be striking gold. Literally.

.

7

FINLEY WATCHED THE truck pull into the cemetery. A burly man climbed out, and even from the back at a distance, something about him seemed familiar. He pulled a large floral wreath out of the bed of his truck and turned toward her. Then she knew. It was Pluto.

She continued her casual search, sneaking glances at him as he left the wreath at a stone. In less than three minutes, he was gone.

When she was sure he'd really driven away, she hurried over to the headstone. It was taller than Finley, wider than her outstretched arms, and larger than any other stone in the cemetery. There were two sections of ornate script carved into it.

The left side read, Marv Jacobsen, 1906–1988.

The words on the right were newer: Madge Jacobsen, 1920–2008. We love you, Mom.

A pleasant aroma came from the yellow and white flowers, and at the bottom was a beaded 11. Finley studied the wreath. It had been more than 11 years since both Marv and Madge died. She racked her brain for any other significance, but the numbers just stared blankly at her.

It obviously marked the grave, but what did the 11 mean? She tilted the wreath forward to look at the back, but all she saw was neatly wrapped floral wire and tape. Letting it fall against the stone, she sighed. She was missing an obvious clue. If only Dale was with her, he would know.

She turned away from the headstone, went down the hill, and left the graveyard. Back in town, she walked slowly up Main Street, hoping Dale or Mrs. Kellogg would be on the porch so she had an excuse to stop. She approached the house slowly, but no one was outside. After standing on the sidewalk deliberating, she climbed the steps and knocked on the door.

Mrs. Kellogg answered the door and gently reminded her that Dale was grounded. The plan formed in Finley's mind instantly and before she knew it, she'd opened her mouth and was asking,

"I know, Mrs. Kellogg, but I was wondering if I could eat dinner here?"

She looked hopefully at Dale's mother. It wasn't only a plot to see Dale, she really was hungry. Mrs. Kellogg's heart went out to the hungry brown eyes of the girl with a snub nose, freckles, and shoulder-length strawberry blonde hair. She didn't hesitate.

"Yes, it's almost ready. Come on in."

Dale was sitting at the kitchen counter bent over a book. When Finley walked in, he looked up curiously. His mother announced,

"Finley is going to eat with us." Dale grinned and motioned to the stool next to him as Mrs. Kellogg continued, "Why don't the two of you go outside until dinner? It'll be ready in five minutes."

Jumping off his stool, Dale said,

"Okay, mom. C'mon Finley, let's play catch." He grabbed his football. As soon as they were on the lawn, Finley said,

"Dale, I found the—"

He interrupted her.

"I'm not supposed to have anything to do with it."

His tone was apologetic and his face was strained, especially after her next words.

"But . . . I need your help."

He didn't reply. They threw the ball in silence until Finley blurted out her question, disregarding Dale's discomfort and rushing through before he could stop her.

"I saw Pluto put a wreath at a grave and I'm assuming that's the grave they'll rob. But the wreath has an eleven on it and I can't figure out what that stands for." Dale laughed as she heaved the ball at him and retorted, "What? Why are you laughing at me?"

He said,

"Finley, remember? He said time and place." She stared at him blankly, so he repeated himself. "The wreath marks the *time and place*."

Finley's mouth dropped open.

"Oh, duh. I'm so dumb."

Dale shook his head.

"Not dumb. Just needed an extra brain."

She made a face and whined,

"But how am I going to catch them all alone?"

"Finley, you need to drop the whole thing. Tell the police you found the time and place, then forget about it. These guys could be seriously dangerous." She didn't respond, so Dale added, "Besides, you never have to be alone. You can ask Jesus to be with you."

Finley grunted.

"I don't understand Jesus. How's he with me? I can't see him."

"Just because you can't see Him doesn't mean he's not there. He's everywhere. It's called being *omnipresent*."

Raising an eyebrow, she said,

"Seems weird. Why would He want to be with me, anyway?"

"Because He loves you."

"He doesn't know me."

Her voice was certain, but Dale shook his head.

"He does. He created you, and He wants you to have a relationship with Him."

Finley frowned. Jesus sounded pretty strange. Before she could ask another question, Mrs. Kellogg called them in for dinner. As they went up the porch stairs, she said,

"He still doesn't make a whole lot of sense to me. What does it mean to have a relationship with him?"

"It means admitting that you're a sinner, then believing that he died for your sins and rose again, and then living your life to please him. It's as simple as talking to him and telling Him you believe in Him and you want to live for Him."

They arrived in the kitchen as he finished, and Finley didn't reply. As soon as she saw the table heaped with delicious looking food, she lost track of the conversation. There was barbecued chicken, mashed potatoes, salad, roasted carrots, and banana pudding for dessert. When dinner was over, Finley thanked Mrs. Kellogg and turned down her offer for a ride. It wasn't dark yet, and Finley still had one stop to make before going home.

She left Dale's house and went down Main Street in the direction of the police station. The door was unlocked when she got there, but Mrs. Toller was gone. Finley looked hopefully through the front desk window and grinned, knocking on the window. David was at his desk looking at something, but he came over when he saw her.

"It's late, Miss Finley. What are you doing here?"

"I figured out the time and the place for the robbery!"

He entered the waiting area.

"I thought I told you not to have anything else to do with it."

Finley shrugged.

"I guess I just stumbled onto it."

She told him about the wreath on the grave. He listened carefully and made a note in his small black notebook:

Marv Jacobsen, Thursday. 2300 hours, Forest Hill Cemetery.

Finley watched him confidently. When he finished writing, he looked at her seriously.

"Now Finley, I really do want you to stay out of this. Criminals don't care if you're a nice young lady. If you get in their way, they will hurt you."

She opened her brown eyes wide and nodded. He grinned and continued.

"Besides, you've already done more than enough to catch these guys. You can leave it to us now. Promise to forget about it?"

She nodded solemnly, but David didn't see her fingers crossed behind her back. Last year she heard that if you cross your fingers behind your back when you're making a promise, you don't have to keep it.

David offered her a ride home and gave her a piece of bubble gum. When they arrived at her house, all the lights were on. Finley grinned. For the first time in weeks, her mom was home before bedtime. She jumped out of the car and ran inside, but her joy dissolved as soon as she entered and saw Steve on one end of the living room and her mother on the other end, both scowling. She tried to sneak past to her bedroom unnoticed, but Steve saw her and said,

"See?!! You can barely raise your own daughter! Do you even know where she's been?"

Finley froze. Her mom motioned toward Finley's room, but Finley didn't move. The red mist that had flooded her mind when Rusty accused her mother rushed in, and without realizing what she was doing, she threw herself at Steve. Short for her age, she stood eye to eye with his chest—so she slammed her fists into his belly, screaming,

"YOU LEAVE MY MOM ALONE!"

Both adults were so surprised that at first neither one reacted. Then Steve held up his arm to deflect her punches and kicked Finley in the shins before her mom could stop him. Startled, Finley fell down as her mother yelled, "DON'T TOUCH HER!" and launched a fist at his face. He yelped and Finley jumped up and pummeled him more, as hard as she could. Steve roared and swung his leg out again, this time landing a knee squarely in Finley's stomach and knocking the wind out of her. She landed on the ground several feet away, but this time she moaned and stayed on the ground.

In a flash, she remembered hitting Rusty in the stomach the day before—and suddenly she felt compassion for him. It really hurt. At that instant, there was a knock on the door.

Steve glared at Finley's mother, who glared back as she walked over and threw open the door. Her defiance softened when she saw David.

"I heard yelling. Is there a problem?"

He leaned his head in and saw Finley whimpering on the floor. Her mother pointed at Steve.

"Yeah. Him."

"What happened to Finley?"

"He kicked her in the stomach."

Steve wasn't going to stand by without defending himself.

"I didn't kick her on purpose! I was raising my knee to protect myself when the little twerp was punching me! She just got the wind knocked out of her."

David cleared his throat and stepped inside. His brawn filled the entryway, and made Steve look much smaller. David looked evenly at the man in the white tank top and baggy gray sweatpants.

"I think you should leave tonight and never come back."

Steve frowned.

"I'm not going anywhere unless Julie tells me to."

Julie, Finley's mother, snorted.

"Fat chance I want you around. Get out."

Steve looked defiantly at David, who added,

"I wasn't giving you a choice."

Julie chimed in again.

"Why would I want you to stay? You're lazy, dirty, rude, good-for-nothing, and mean. Leave and never come back."

Steve's face got red and he muttered some curse words and directed a few impolite parting remarks at Finley's mom. Then he picked up a sweatshirt and stalked out, brushing past David.

The whole scenario took less than five minutes, from Finley's first screaming leap to Steve's angry exit. Finley's mother turned to David.

"Thank you."

He nodded. After David left, Finley's mother turned off the TV and sat on the couch for a long time, staring at the black screen and sighing every few minutes. Finley sat down next to her mother and hugged her tightly. She was drifting off to sleep when her mother broke the silence.

"I'm sorry. I messed up pretty bad, didn't I?"

Finley mumbled,

"It's okay. Maybe you'll do better next time."

Tears silently rolled down Julie's face as she held onto her drowsy daughter, stroking her hair. She resolved that there would be no "next time."

.

ON WEDNESDAY MORNING, Finley woke up when her mom got off the couch to leave for work. When she came back into the living room, she kissed Finley on the head and asked,

"Would you like to make cookies together when I get home from work tonight?"

Finley eagerly answered.

"Yes!"

She was late to school because her stomach was sore and it hurt to run. When she was signing in at the office, Mrs. Jackson, the administrative assistant, asked why she was late. Finley shrugged. Mrs. Jackson looked over her wrinkled clothes and messy hair and raised an eyebrow. Finley wasn't usually this sloppy.

As soon as Dale saw her, he asked,

"What happened?"

She summarized the night before. When she told him how David made Steve leave, Dale grinned.

"Cool."

Finley shrugged.

"Yeah, I guess it kind of was."

Determined to make it through the day without a detention, Finley worked hard to sit still and keep her mouth shut in Mr. Slinch's class. All she wanted to do was get home and make cookies with her mom. When Rusty Cowell teased her about her looks, she stared straight ahead and pretended his voice was a dog barking.

As soon as the bell rang at the end of the day, she bolted out. On their walk home she told Dale more about what happened. He asked,

"So Steve really isn't coming back?"

"I hope not. But I guess that's what I thought the day before yesterday too, and he was back. So I guess we'll see."

When they reached her street, she said,

"I'm not coming over for dinner today. My mom said she'd make cookies with me after work."

She turned down her street, and Dale breathed a sigh of relief as he watched her go. Tomorrow was Thursday. All day, Dale had been careful not to mention the robbery. He knew she hadn't given up, but he hoped that maybe her time with her mom would make her drop the whole thing. After she left his house the night before, his parents lectured him again about how dangerous it could be to get mixed up with criminals. Deep down, he knew they were right.

The house was empty when Finley got home. She ate a snack and did her homework, then sat on the front steps.

Soon, she was bored, so she found her jump rope and jumped rope up and down the street, but soon she got tired. Then she found her old sidewalk chalk in the hall closet and drew on the sidewalk.

As the shadows grew longer, Finley got hungry. It was six thirty-five and her mom still wasn't home, so she microwaved a tv dinner. The chicken strips were rubbery and the cheesy potatoes didn't taste as good as the cheesy potatoes Dale's mom made last week, but it was better than being hungry. When she finished eating, it was seven o'clock. Finley assumed her mom must have just worked some extra hours.

Finley went back outside and sat on the porch with her chin in her hands, imagining what it would be like if her mom was like Mrs. Kellogg. There would be regular meals, she would always be home when Finley got home from school, and there wouldn't be a different boyfriend every few months. A police car cruising slowly down the street stopped in front of her house and interrupted her wishful thinking.

David got out of the car.

"These are beautiful chalk drawings, Miss Pike." Finley shrugged. "What're you doing out here?"

She explained her mom's promise after the fight last night. David knew the first shift left the factory several hours ago, but he didn't say that. Instead, he reached into his pocket for a piece of gum, handed it to Finley, and asked,

"Mind if I sit down?" She shrugged again. He lowered himself onto the step next to her, grunting. "When you get old like me, it's not so easy to get to the ground."

No response. Her chin was back in her hands and she was staring at the street. After a long silence, she said,

"I don't think my mom is coming home to make cookies."

David hated that Finley was probably right.

"I'm sorry."

They stayed there in silence until David got a call and left, and Finley sat by herself on the step in the dark. When she started to feel sleepy she went inside, crawled into bed, and sobbed.

Several hours after her daughter cried herself to sleep, Finley's mother stumbled into the house. She bumped into the table in the kitchen and tripped over the rug in the hallway, falling to the floor. She crawled into the bathroom, vomited into the toilet, and fumbled her way back out to the living room, where she fell asleep on the couch with her shoes on.

And that's where she was the next morning when Finley came into the living room to leave for school. Finley nudged her shoulder.

"Mom? Mom? Mom, wake up. You have to go to work."

Her mom opened bleary eyes and blinked at her daughter.

"Is it morning already?" She lifted her head, but groaned and quickly lowered it. Finley nodded and left without another word. She walked to school again. Her stomach was still sore and her heart was heavy.

When Dale saw her in the hall before class, he immediately asked,

"What's wrong?"

"My mom didn't come home in time to make cookies."

"Oh."

"So I sat at home alone until I went to bed."

"Remember how I told you that you never have to be alone?"

Finley shrugged.

"It doesn't feel like it helps if it's someone I can't see who can't talk to me or make cookies with me."

Dale cocked his head to one side.

"Yeah, I know it feels that way. But He really is with you and He really does love you, even though you can't see Him."

Finley frowned.

"Jesus doesn't make any sense." She thought back to their last conversation, remembering Dale's comment about Jesus dying and coming back to life. "Besides, how could he die and rise again? That seems weird. Is He a zombie?"

Dale laughed, but stopped when he realized Finley's question was sincere.

"No, he's alive again, just like you and me."

Finley frowned.

"That really doesn't make a lot of sense, Dale."

Dale nodded and replied,

"I know. But Jesus could do it because He's God."

"So Jesus is always with me, He rose from the dead, and He's God, too?"

"Yep."

"That's crazy. How do you believe all this stuff?"

Dale thought carefully for a minute before he answered.

"Because I know it's true."

"But how?"

"The Bible is true, and it tells me all about Jesus and God. Besides that, I talk to Him every day and I see ways that He works in my life."

Just then the bell rang, and they parted ways for their first class of the day. When she got to class, Finley sank into her seat and dropped her head to her desk. The conversation with Dale left her confused, and she was still absorbed in sadness from the night before.

Miss Maven, the art teacher, was grumpy most of the time, but she loved Thursdays. As class began, she sang out in a lyrical voice,

"Good morning, students! Before we get started today, I'd like to show off this beautiful watercolor of wildflowers that Finley completed earlier this week."

Finley's head snapped up off her desk. Miss Maven was one of the few teachers who didn't seem to mind Finley's surplus of energy, and she was always encouraging everything that Finley created. Now, she held a piece of watercolor paper high and explained to the class why it was so well done. Her words warmed Finley down to her toes. She sat straight, grinning. Teachers barely ever praised her. It felt nice.

When Miss Maven finished talking about Finley's painting, she set it down on her desk and continued,

"And now, Hah-pp-eey Thursday! Let's get creating!"

Finley jumped. It was Thursday! She'd been so distracted about her mom that she'd forgotten all about the grave robbers.

Tonight was the night.

9

"BUT WE CAN'T just do nothing."

It was more of a whine than a statement. Dale took another bite of his ham sandwich before answering.

"We have to trust the police."

Finley held a chicken nugget in one hand and a plastic spoon heaping with baked beans in the other. She shrugged. Sure, David was helpful—after all, he got rid of Steve. But she couldn't shake the feeling that he hadn't believed their tip about the robbery.

Mitchell Fitzwell had developed the habit of pushing his cart close behind them during lunch. Today he looked closely at Finley as she spoke, then determined he would try to talk to her soon.

Dean walked over with his lunch bag and settled in next to Finley. He pushed his big brown glasses up his nose and peered at her.

"You okay?"

She sighed and shrugged. Dale waited in nervous silence to hear if her answer would be about her mom or the robbery. Dean picked up his sandwich and took a bite before Finley answered.

"I just had a bad day yesterday and I'm having another bad day today."

"I'm sorry." He pushed a cellophane packet over to her and added, "You can have my brownie."

She gratefully accepted the dessert.

"Thanks, Dean."

He nodded, and Dale looked at him appreciatively. Then he changed the subject.

"Today in music we learned a new song on our buckets." The music class enrichment was six weeks long, and so far after five weeks the only thing they'd done was watch musicals and use drumsticks to beat out song rhythms on plastic five-gallon buckets. He continued, "After two weeks of doing *Mary Had a Little Lamb*, I guess Mrs. Martin decided we were experienced enough for something else. We graduated to *Twinkle, Twinkle Little Star.*"

Finley grunted around a mouthful of brownie, but her mind wandered back to the graveyard. She wondered if the robbers were really going to dig tonight. When Dale asked, "Don't you think so? Finley?" She jolted back to the present and said,

"Oh. Sure."

Dale frowned, and Dean said,

"Really? Wow. I wouldn't have guessed that."

She looked back and forth between the two of them, but the bell saved her from admitting she didn't know what she'd just agreed to. They all stood and gathered their trays, and Dale whispered,

"Please stop thinking about it, Finley."

She didn't respond.

That afternoon in Mrs. O'Malley's class, Finley had trouble concentrating on *The Adventures of Tom Sawyer*. Her mind kept wandering back to the graveyard.

After school she walked out with Dale, who invited her over for dinner. Finley nodded.

"I'm sure my mom won't come home till late again anyways."

Her voice was sad. They walked together till Finley turned on her street to go home. After changing out of her school clothes, she sat on the front steps and ate a bowl of cereal—but being there alone reminded her of the night before, so as soon as she finished eating, Finley walked to the cemetery. The wreath was exactly where Pluto left it two days earlier. As she stared at it, she rehearsed her plan.

After dark, she would come back to the cemetery and hide behind a gravestone. When she saw the robbers, she would watch them so she could be a witness after the police arrested them. It all seemed so simple. She walked around looking around for a good place to hide.

A few rows away from Marv's plot, she found a long granite bench. She crawled under it and was pleased to find that when she was on her side, she could bend her legs and be completely concealed by the large stone slab.

The fine grass under the bench was refreshingly cool in the warm September air, and a few surrounding gravestones sheltered Finley from the cool fall wind. Closing her eyes, she imagined what would happen tonight—after catching the criminals, she would be celebrated by the whole town. Maybe her mom would want to be with her more if she became a Malvern celebrity. Maybe she would stop looking for the next boyfriend and just be content with their life. Maybe . . .

Finley's eyes flew open. She was cold. Groaning, Finley realized she'd fallen asleep. It was dusk. Rolling out from under the bench, her first thought was disappointment that she might have missed dinner at Dale's house. She took off at a slow run, not pushing her sore stomach. As she hurried up Main Street, she saw a familiar truck parked in front of the old jewelry store. Pluto came out, and when he saw her he frowned. After a moment he shook his head and climbed into his truck, watching her run up Main Street.

When Finley reached Dale's house, he was outside waiting for her.

"Where were you? You missed dinner." She nodded but didn't answer. He scrutinized her, noticing the marks on her cheek where grass had pressed against it. He asked again. "Where were you?"

"I fell asleep in the grass."

Dale watched her shuffle her feet and let the subject drop. Finley didn't say much while she gulped down her chicken pot pie, cheesy rice, salad, and banana pudding. After dinner, Mrs. Kellogg offered her a ride home. Once in the car, she said,

"I'm sorry about your mom."

Silence from the passenger seat. Finley figured Dale must have told them about her mom not coming home the night before. Mrs. Kellogg didn't press, though. Instead, she said,

"Finley, it's very dangerous to get involved with criminals."

"Yeah."

Dale's mom continued, explaining that they wouldn't care about being kind to her, even if she was young. But Finley wasn't listening. She was thinking through her plan for the night and wondering if her mom would be home. When they pulled into her short driveway, Finley sighed. The house was dark. As Finley climbed out of the car, Mrs. Kellogg said,

"Call if you need anything!"

Finley nodded, not bothering to tell Mrs. Kellogg that the house phone was disconnected months ago when her mother didn't pay the bill. She went straight to her room and rummaged through her dresser to find dark clothes. The pants she found were too short and she had to turn the black hoodie inside out to hide the bright white flower on the front, but she was satisfied she'd be hard to see in the dark.

After she put them on, she sat on her bed and watched the time. The green LED numbers on her small bedroom clock seemed to stand still at 8:04, and she sighed with dread at the thought of waiting for the next hour and a half. She reached into her backpack for the homework Mr. Slinch had handed out that morning. They'd moved on from tides since last week, and now they were studying types of rock. She hurried through the worksheet then settled onto her bed and looked at the ceiling.

A car passed on the quiet street, and the small old house creaked as it settled. For at least the tenth time that day, she thought through every step of her plan, starting with sneaking out of the house at nine thirty. Then she tried to read a book, but just stared at the words on the page. Nothing could keep her attention, and even after her accidental nap, she was still so tired. Maybe she could just rest her eyes for a minute.

For the second time that day, she woke up with a jolt. It was ten fifteen. She groaned.

"Not again."

Leaping off the bed, she scrambled into her shoes and eased her door open. A peek into the hall showed pitch darkness. Her mom still wasn't home. Creeping down the hallway toward the front door, she walked as softly as possible. Once outside, she pulled the door closed behind her and stood on the tiny cement porch. It was dark, except for Mr. Arthwell's porch light and the glimmer of streetlights on Main Street, two blocks away.

Finley had been outside by herself during the night at home, but she'd never gone through town by herself this late. She shivered and put up the hood on her sweatshirt. The shadows seemed larger than life, and she jumped when a nearby dog started barking. Hurrying down the three cement stairs, she started off at a run toward Main Street. Her sore stomach hurt with every step, but she didn't have time to go slow. Lifting her eyes from the sidewalk in front of her, she looked around and immediately regretted it.

Bushes looked more like bears—toys that children had left out looked like little monsters creeping toward her on the sidewalk, and Finley's overactive imagination saw someone sinister looming behind every tree. Her heart raced and she looked back down at the sidewalk. She only looked up at the houses one more time, as she ran past Dale's house. There were lights on in the living room. Soon she was on the business stretch of Main Street. All the stores were dark, and the street lamps cast pools of light in intervals on the sidewalk. When she saw a car turn up Main Street, she instinctively ducked into the entryway of a building and crouched down. It passed, but she waited until it had gone several blocks before emerging from her hiding spot and continuing south.

Not a car was in sight on the dark highway as Finley jogged across it. In another block she was at the dark trail, and her stomach jumped into her throat. Disregarding the pangs in her stomach, she started to run again. It seemed much farther than it had earlier in the day, and every rustle in the bushes made her leap forward.

When she finally reached the cemetery road, she turned onto it and ran in the ditch. Lights on a house further down the road reassured her. The side of the cemetery ran along this road, and she had one more turn to make to come in through the main entrance—but before she'd reached it, she heard a car coming on the dirt road behind her. She crouched in the ditch, pulling her hood tighter around her face and watching the headlights approach. It was a big vehicle crawling slowly along. When it was even with her, she saw that it was a pickup truck, but not just any pickup truck. It was Pluto's truck.

After it passed her, she started moving again, but a moment later the truck stopped. Finley dropped to the ground in terror. Pluto had seen her!

Crouching, she scrambled out of the ditch into the field and crawled toward the trees on the edge of the field, no longer afraid that someone might be hiding in them. She was more afraid of Pluto. Her palms were scratched by the rough stalks and she felt both knees of her sweatpants rip as the stalks tore into them, but she didn't slow her frantic pace.

After what felt like miles, she reached the woods and flattened herself against a tree. Craning her neck to look around it, she studied the field. No one was there. Maybe he hadn't seen her after all. She checked the time. It was 10:40. She began to notice the night noises, and as she became used to them she heard a sound that didn't belong. It was the *click* of a car door closing gently.

Straining her eyes in the darkness, she squinted at the truck. Maybe it was her imagination, but she could just barely make out a figure walking away from it, toward the cemetery. Her heart was pounding. Would she be able to sneak in if he was already there?

She waited until she couldn't see him anymore, then she crept forward. Instead of going through the front entrance like she'd planned, she'd have to sneak in through the back. But if she didn't hurry, the others might arrive and completely ruin her chances of making it to her hiding place. For all she knew, they might already be there.

Working her way back through the field to the road, she crossed to the opposite ditch and followed it to the back corner of the cemetery. There was a short stone wall enclosing the cemetery, and when she reached it, Finley crouched against it and peered over.

She remembered the general area of the bench she would hide under—but she'd have to go past Marv's grave to reach it, and she wasn't sure where Pluto was. She'd have to take a chance. Drawing a deep breath, Finley eased over the wall, crawled up behind a large gravestone, and hunched behind it. Now she was barely breathing.

Peeking around the stone, she looked for any movement. Nothing moved in the darkness. She crawled toward a big square slab in the next row and looked around it. Not seeing anything, she moved to the next row. Stone by stone, it was a slow process. But according to her calculations, she was almost to her bench.

Pressed up against a particularly large gravestone, she froze. Footsteps rustled in the grass and stopped on the other side of it. She didn't breathe. After a prolonged pause, the owner of the footsteps moved on. Finley slowly looked around the corner of her hiding spot and watched a large man step away into the darkness.

As she crawled around the edge of the stone, her breath caught in her chest. A wreath was leaning on the gravestone she'd just been hiding behind. It was Marv Jacobsen's grave.

Finley crawled as fast as she could to the next row of stones, blood pounding in her ears. The distance between rows seemed so far. After what felt like a mile, but was really only several rows, she was safely hidden under her bench—and not a moment too soon. In the darkness, she could discern a figure approaching Marv's stone, and suddenly the peaceful silence was broken by a shrill whistle. Almost immediately several other figures materialized from all different directions in the darkness.

Finley's blood ran cold. What if they were there all along? What if they'd seen her?

10

FINLEY WATCHED AS the black-clad group started digging. She hoped this meant they didn't know she was there.

The only sound was the occasional clink of metal against rock, and the *swish* of dirt falling on the ground. From her hiding spot, Finley counted them. She could make out seven people, six digging in close quarters and one person keeping watch. They had no lights, so she couldn't see any faces.

After a while, Finley began to wonder why the police hadn't shown up. They should have been here by now. She wondered if she should sneak out of the graveyard and run to town to warn them, but she was afraid to creep out from under her bench. The person keeping watch continually turned, looking in every direction, and she felt sure they would see her if she moved. She racked her brain for another idea.

A short time earlier, chaos had broken out in town.

It started when Dale entered his parents' bedroom while they were getting ready for bed. Mr. Kellogg, toothbrush in his mouth, garbled from the bathroom,

"What's wrong, Dale? You're supposed to be in sleeping."

Mrs. Kellogg had just finished washing her face and was laying against big pillows on the bed. She asked,

"Is everything okay?"

He shook his head.

"I think Finley is going to the cemetery."

Mrs. Kellogg said,

"I talked to her about it in the car. She seemed to understand it was a bad idea." Dale wasn't convinced. She continued, "Would it make you feel better if I called to make sure she's home?"

Dale nodded. Mrs. Kellogg found Finley's phone number in an old phone book. After dialing and listening for a second, she pulled the phone away from her ear, frowning.

"It's been disconnected."

Mr. Kellogg, who had spit out his mouthful of toothpaste, said,

"She's probably fine."

Dale shook his head again.

"I don't think she ever gave up on the whole thing."

The Kellogg parents had raised their children to tell the truth, so when one of their children was sure about something, the parents took them seriously to respect them. Mrs. Kellogg asked,

"Would it make you feel better if dad went over and checked on her?"

Dale nodded. Mr. Kellogg left the room, and a moment later they heard his car start and pull out of the driveway. Mrs. Kellogg and Dale sat on the bed in silence. Both of them jumped when the phone rang a few minutes later. After Mr. Kellogg's first words, Mrs. Kellogg asked,

"What should we do?"

When she hung up, she turned to Dale.

"Finley's not home. Her mom didn't know it until dad asked about her." Dale wasn't surprised. His mother continued, "She's pretty upset. Dad's going to come get you, and the two of you can look for her. Go put some clothes on."

As soon as his dad pulled into the driveway, Dale hurried out and got into the car. His dad asked,

"Any ideas?"

"The graveyard."

Not long before, Finley was running past their house—but now she was huddled under a granite bench watching seven stealthy figures, trying to figure out how to sneak out of her hiding spot without being seen.

At first Finley didn't see the headlights, she just heard another shrill whistle like the first one. She craned her neck to see better. One digger produced a dark sheet and spread it over the developing hole. By the time bright headlight beams swung past Finley, the entire group had vanished.

It was the police! It was about time. She laid as still as possible and craned her neck, but all she could see were headlights passing between stones. The car rounded the back side of the cemetery slowly, and for a second it looked like it would keep going. Finley willed the car to stop with all her might—and when all hope seemed lost, suddenly it did. She heard the engine shut off and two car doors slam, and she waited eagerly for the bright police flashlight beam to shine across the grass. Instead, she heard a familiar voice.

"Ah, shoot! I forgot my flashlight."

Finley couldn't believe her ears. It was Mr. Kellogg. What was he doing here? The answer came through Dale's anxious yell.

"Finley!!! Where are you? Please come out!"

Finley's heart sank. They would blow her cover. She didn't move, didn't blink, didn't breathe. If she came out while Dale and Mr. Kellogg were there, the robbers would be forced to leave her alone, for now—but they'd know who she was, and she wouldn't be safe. Mr. Kellogg said,

"Maybe we should just walk around to see if she fell asleep or something."

She waited in terror as they approached. If they kept walking toward her, they would stumble right into the partially excavated grave site. All this time she'd been afraid the robbers would see her, but she knew it could be just as bad, maybe worse, if Dale and Mr. Kellogg found the robbers. Finley's mind raced. If only she could make them go a different direction. But before she thought of an idea she heard a faint voice calling,

"Over here, guys! Over here!"

Dale said,

"Dad, did you hear that?"

They abruptly changed course, heading for the far end of the cemetery. Finley breathed a quiet sigh of relief as their voices faded, but it wasn't long before she heard them approaching again.

"That was strange. Maybe we just imagined it."

Mr. Kellogg replied with uncertainty.

"Maybe . . ."

Dale still sounded hopeful, but there was finality in Mr. Kellogg's tone when he spoke again.

"Well, she's not here. Where else should we look?"

After a pause, Dale answered,

"Sometimes she stays at the playground pretty late. Maybe she went there after mom dropped her off. She might not have wanted to go home after last night."

Last night replayed in an instant in Finley's mind, and it renewed her resolve to catch these crooks. When she was a hero, her mom would definitely want to spend time with her.

As Dale and Mr. Kellogg moved toward their car, Finley let herself breathe. Even though she would've liked nothing better than to crawl out from under her stone and go with them, she was relieved that they were leaving. It meant her cover wasn't blown—at least, not yet. After the car drove out of the cemetery, the dark figures reappeared and kept digging. She watched as the pile of dirt grew. Before long, Finley could only see the diggers from their waists up. She guessed that soon they'd pull the casket out of the ground, and she frowned. Why weren't the police coming? She had no choice but to sneak away and run back to town to tell them. Finley was edging out of her hiding spot when someone broke the silence with a quiet yell.

The diggers all stopped, and Finley peered through the darkness. They'd hit the casket. She couldn't leave now.

11

AS SOON AS FINLEY'S mother realized Finley was gone, a humiliating discovery to make with Mr. Kellogg standing at her front door, she called the police to report her missing child. The Malvern Police Department only kept one squad car on overnight duty, and in spite of Finley's warnings, there was only one officer working tonight: Phil, a short, skinny man with buck teeth, thinning hair, and a penchant for overreaction.

When the dispatcher radioed about a missing child, Phil hurried over to Finley's house to talk to her mother, who was close to hysterics. For someone who didn't know where her child was on a regular basis, she was very concerned about Finley's current status.

Finley's mom opened the door and greeted the officer, who nodded politely and stepped into the entryway, exactly where David stood two evenings earlier. He got right to the point, ignoring her tears.

"Julie. When was the last time you saw Finley?"

She sheepishly admitted that she'd only seen her briefly that morning, and not at all the day before. He nodded, jotting this down in his small notebook. She didn't know where Finley usually spent her time, she didn't have any idea where she might be, and she was beside herself with concern. When Phil had no more questions, he said,

"She might come back on her own. A lot of runaway kids do. Stay here, and I'll have a look around town."

Phil left and Julie resumed her nervous pacing. Her thoughts tormented her as she remembered her dad saying that someday her negligence would catch up to her.

"I guess it's catching up to me," she mumbled, crying into her hands.

After Phil left Finley's house, he went to the middle school playground. He was shining his flashlight up a slide when the dispatcher radioed him again. Someone had just reported lights inside the local bank. Phil asked the dispatcher to contact backup and hurried back to his car. Finley, wherever she was, would have to wait.

Phil parked a block away from the bank and crept toward it. When he arrived, he circled the building on tiptoe, peering through the windows. He passed three sides of the building without seeing anything out of the ordinary, but on the fourth side, as he looked through the window, he froze. There was a shadowy figure inside, creeping around with a flashlight. Phil sank to the ground, radioing dispatch again to tell them to hurry with the backup. Heart pounding, he looked inside and whispered a quiet prayer that someone would show up soon.

In the meantime, things were going well for the SODD at Marv Jacobsen's tomb. They struck wood with a dull *thump* and a yell soon after Dale and Mr. Kellogg left. Even from her hiding spot, Finley could feel their excitement increasing. They continued to dig cautiously, and before long one of the diggers gave a signal. Finley heard muffled grunting and watched as they straightened, holding the long dark shape. Easing it over the edge of the hole, they rested it on the grass.

The person who hadn't done any digging crouched in front of the coffin, while the diggers sat around it. Finley was crawling out from under the bench to sneak back to town when she heard a loud 'click.' She froze, terrified it might be a gun, but then she realized it was the coffin lock clicking into the unlocked position. Hiding behind the bench, she watched as several of the black-clad figures lifted the lid.

For a moment, there was dead silence—then the peaceful scene abruptly ended.

Three of the diggers jumped up as the lid slammed closed. Finley heard the low rumble of sudden argument, but she couldn't tell what they were saying. She frowned and was thinking about sneaking closer to hear their words when the person who opened the coffin said, "Stop!"

Finley didn't need to see a face to recognize the voice. It was Pluto, speaking in a tone that would take no disagreement. Desperate to hear his words, Finley crept toward the group. Now, less than 15 feet away, she could finally understand what he said.

"Just because the body is missing doesn't mean there's not a logical explanation." Finley gave a quiet gasp as he continued. "I'm sure the ghost isn't wandering around in the graveyard. Obviously, this plot hasn't been disturbed for years, and there's a logical explanation for all of this. But now is not the time to worry about it. Now is the time to finish the job and get out of here."

One of the figures took a step back, saying,

"I'm out. I don't want to take money from a ghost."

A few of them nodded in agreement, and chills ran down Finley's spine. A ghost? Was Marv's ghost haunting the graveyard and plotting revenge against everyone there, including her?

Pluto answered,

"You know how this works. You agreed from the day you signed up. You know the risks. You don't get a choice."

A woman piped up,

"But this has never happened."

The murmurs began again, but Pluto stopped them right away.

"Who is in charge here?"

After a moment of silence, Finley heard a meek voice. She recognized it from the jewelry store as Minnie's.

"You are."

The rest of the group murmured in agreement.

"That's right. And I say that we are going to finish this job, body or not. And if any of you disagree with me . . ." He paused, then pointed at the coffin. "That won't be empty when we bury it. And you won't be dead."

Paralyzed by his words, no one said a word.

"Well, what are you waiting for? Let's finish."

He stepped forward and opened the coffin. They lifted out two large bags that Finley assumed contained the gold.

For the first time in the whole operation, Pluto turned on a flashlight as he opened the bags. Finley could hear his purr of satisfaction as he muttered,

"Good job, old man. Good job."

Then he flipped off his light and said,

"Time to fill in the hole."

Finley watched in dismay as the group lowered the casket back into the ground and started covering it with dirt. Maybe the police really weren't coming, and now it was too late to get them. The hole would be full before she could get to town.

Suddenly, she realized there was another problem. When they finished, they would have to pass her to get to the road—and someone was bound to see her. She had to get out. Now.

She crept backward, passing stones one row at a time, and hurrying across the open patches of grass. When she was close enough to the entrance, she hunched over and ran toward it.

Just a few rows away from the open gate, she stopped short and dropped to the ground. She couldn't be certain, but it looked like there was a large vehicle parked on the side of the road right next to the entrance. It was probably Goofy with the getaway car. What if he'd already seen her?

Stuck between the van on one side and the robbers on the other side, Finley turned to the right and ducked along the row of gravestones, toward the edge of the cemetery that bordered the road she came in on. When she finally reached the low wall, she rolled over it, slipped into the ditch, and took off running. Before long, she was back at the trail.

It was still pitch black, but the run back to town seemed much shorter than the run to the graveyard. Now that the adrenaline was wearing off, she started to feel pain in her stomach again. When she reached South Main Street, Finley slowed to a walk. At the intersection of Main Street and the highway, she was surprised to see flashing red and blue lights. There were three police cars pulled up in front of the bank on the far corner. She crossed the highway on the other side of the intersection, trying to avoid being seen, but when she was halfway across, an officer yelled and came running.

"Finley? Finley Pike?"

He was tense and hyper. She nodded quietly, aware that she was breaking town curfew—people under 16 aren't supposed to be out without an adult after the streetlights come on. The streetlights came on hours ago. Nodding sheepishly, she said,

"Yeah."

"I'm officer Phil. I've been looking for you—well, I was, before the bank . . ."

His voice faded as she looked curiously at him.

"Looking for me?"

"Your mom called in that you were missing a few hours ago."

Warmth washed over Finley's whole body. Her mom was looking for her. Phil was still talking, but Finley wasn't paying attention anymore. Maybe things really were finally changing. Phil interrupted her silent delight.

"Are you listening to me? Where were you? Surely you know the rules about curfew."

Finley didn't answer his questions—instead, she asked,

"What happened at the bank? I told the police about the robbery. You were supposed to be watching the graveyard."

Phil shuffled his feet. David had mentioned this when he came in for his shift, but in the frenzy of Finley missing and the bank holdup, Phil forgot about it.

"We're not talking about the bank, that's none of your business. And that whole graveyard thing sounded too ridiculous to be true."

Finley frowned.

"Ridiculous? I watched a group of people rob a grave. I even told David they were going to be there, and nobody came!" Her voice grew louder and became shrill. "And the coffin was empty but the gold was still in it, and they took the gold and reburied the empty coffin!"

Phil raised an eyebrow.

"That's quite the story."

Stomping her foot, Finley said,

"It's not just a story, it happened! I saw! We might still be able to catch them if we hurry."

Phil shook his head.

"The only place you're going to hurry to is home. After I drop you off I'll go check it out myself."

Finley knew she wouldn't get anywhere by arguing. She was worried he wouldn't be able to find the grave without her, but him going alone was better than him not going at all.

"Okay, but make sure you bring a flashlight." She explained where Marv's grave was, and said, "If they're still there, they'll be hiding somewhere around it. Don't leave without finding it."

Phil led her to his squad car, which was parked near the bank. When they got close to the building, Finley saw a small group of policemen come through the front doors. One of them said,

"I just don't get it. He got away from Phil, but he didn't take anything."

She stopped in her tracks and said,

"He got away from you?"

Phil opened the car door and motioned inside, muttering,

"We're not talking about it."

As soon as they pulled into Finley's driveway, her mom rushed out of the house. She took Finley into her arms and held her while Phil stood there in awkward silence.

After going over the events of the evening with the pair, Phil left. He promised Finley that he would check out the graveyard, but by the time he gathered a group and drove out, it was too late. Everyone was gone. Even though he found Marv's grave, in the dark it didn't look disturbed.

He shook his head. Crazy kid, wasting my time.

12

FINLEY WAS BACK IN the graveyard watching the diggers when one of them spotted her. Forming a circle around her, they chanted,

"Put her in the coffin, put her in the coffin, put her in the coffin!"

They were closing in when her alarm went off.

She rolled over and pulled the blankets over her head as the events of the night before flooded through her mind. They got away. She couldn't believe it. Unless Phil caught them when he went to the graveyard, she'd failed. Well, almost. The look on her mom's face when she threw open the door kept coming back to her. Maybe she didn't have to catch criminals for her mom to care about her. Maybe she did care, she was just bad at showing it.

When she saw Dale in the hallway at school, he yelled,

"Finley!" He ran over and his words poured out. "We looked for you last night but we couldn't find you. We went home and prayed that you would be okay. Where were you?"

Dale narrowed his eyes at her as she looked at her feet.

"Sorry."

He groaned.

"Aw man, Finley. You were there when we came looking for you? Even after my parents and David told you not to go so many times?"

She nodded, and said feebly,

"I had to." She didn't say that she had to because she was hoping it would make her mom love her more and want to spend more time with her. Dale frowned and she went on. "And I was right about the police. They never came. The robbers got away."

Finley and Dale were standing outside of Dale's first class, and Mitchell Fitzwell slowly rolled a trash can past. He stopped when she mentioned the police and the graveyard. Dale said,

"The police didn't come because they were looking for you."

His voice carried the sting of accusation, but Finley defended herself.

"No, Phil said they were chasing the person who was trying to rob the bank on Main Street."

Dale felt a twinge of guilt as he remembered Pluto's words from the jewelry store meeting: Gas station, maybe? Or bank? We need a solid two hours, depending on how many volunteers we get.

"Oh yeah. I forgot about that."

The bell rang, and Finley bolted down the almost empty hallway. Mitchell Fitzwell watched her thoughtfully. Could it be that this energetic girl had accidentally stumbled upon the ring of criminals he'd been trying to find for almost two years?

Later that morning, Finley was sitting in Mr. Slinch's science class, staring at a spot on the wall above the whiteboard. Suddenly, Mrs. Jackson's voice blared over the intercom.

"Finley Pike, please come to the office."

Finley lurched back to the present at the sound of her name. She usually only got called to the office when she was in trouble. Confused, she looked at Dale. He shrugged. Mr. Slinch wrote her a pass and she walked slowly down the hall. When she got to the office, she was surprised to see that Mrs. Jackson didn't look annoyed like she usually did when she called Finley to the office. In fact, she was smiling.

"Someone dropped off a note for you."

No one had ever left Finley a note at school. Mrs. Jackson handed it to her and watched intently, but Finley took it and walked out. She didn't want to share this special moment—whatever it might be—with Mrs. Jackson. Adults never knew when to be quiet in special moments.

As soon as she was in the hallway, she tore the envelope open. Inside was a yellow lined piece of paper. Finley stopped dead in her tracks when she read the words.

We know you were there last night. If you tell anyone what you saw, we'll put you in the empty coffin.—Malvern SODD

Finley was so absorbed in her terror that she didn't notice the jingle of keys behind her. She jumped when someone asked,

"Everything all right, Miss Pike?"

Spinning around, she looked up into Mitchell Fitzwell's friendly face.

"Oh, Mister Fitzwell. Yeah, it's fine."

He narrowed his eyes. She was holding the note at an angle, and he could see the large handwriting scrawled across it, right down to the signature. It confirmed all his suspicions.

"I want to talk to you after school, if you'll have a few minutes."

"I guess."

"Great. I'll meet you outside of your classroom."

Finley walked back to class at a snail's pace, mind racing. How did they know she was there? Who could she tell? What if they found out she'd already told the police?

Her nightmare seemed to be coming true.

13

AFTER WATCHING FINLEY pick at her food, Dale said,

"What's the matter? It's not your fault."

She shook her head.

"It's not that."

They hadn't told Dean about the grave robbers, and now he looked curiously between the two of them.

"What's not her fault?"

Neither spoke for a moment, then Dale said,

"She tried to catch robbers last night and they got away."

Dean blinked.

"Oh."

Finley said,

"That's not why I'm upset."

Both boys looked confused. Dean asked,

"It's not? What's wrong?"

She shrugged. Dale prompted,

"Come on, Finley."

Finley slowly reached for the note that she'd crumpled up and stuffed into her pocket. Dale read it, frowning.

"You need to tell David."

She was incredulous.

"The police didn't take me seriously before, why would they now?"

"Because you're in danger. Something could happen to you."

She shoved the note back into her pocket, shrugging coolly. It wasn't how she felt, but she wanted them to think she was brave.

Dean asked,

"How did you get into this mess?"

They told him the whole story. Then Finley told them about seeing Mitchell Fitzwell when she got the note and how he wanted to talk to her after class. Dale asked,

"Do you think it's related?"

"I don't know. But will you come with me? I'm afraid it could be a trap from the SODD."

Dale nodded and Dean sighed.

"I wish I could come too. I have to go to the eye doctor after school. You'll have to tell me how it went tomorrow at my party." The bell rang, and Dean pulled two envelopes out of his backpack. "Here are your invitations."

When her last class of the day ended, Finley hurried out and almost bumped right into Mitchell, who was standing outside the classroom with a broom and a trash can. He grinned at her and motioned for her to follow him, but she said,

"Dale's coming too."

Mitchell nodded. As Finley's classmates streamed out of the doorway, they looked at Mitchell with wide eyes. They still believed he was a magician. Then Dale appeared, and they followed Mitchell down a long, abandoned hallway toward the janitor's closet.

He stopped in front of the closet and pulled a large ring of keys from his belt. Finley drew back nervously, but when he swung the door open her curiosity pushed her forward. She half expected to see a magician's garb hanging in the small closet, but it just held typical janitorial items: a mop, a few brooms, bottles of cleaning supplies, a cleaning cart, some buckets, and rolls and rolls of toilet paper.

Mitchell pulled three buckets into the hallway and turned them over, motioning for Finley and Dale to sit, and he did the same. Then, looking straight at them, he said,

"Tell me exactly what happened."

Finley looked at Dale, who was studying Mitchell carefully. After a moment he nodded slowly.

"He's okay."

She launched into the story, starting with the jewelry store. Dale added details occasionally, and Mitchell interrupted with questions, particularly when Finley talked about the corn maze. He seemed to care mostly that they'd seen Pluto's face and asked if they could identify him if they saw him again. When she showed him the note, he frowned and muttered.

"That's low."

After they finished, Mitchell was quiet for a moment. These unsuspecting high schoolers had stumbled onto one of the biggest active crime rings in the state. Finley, relieved that she'd made it through the whole story without getting turned into a frog or a rabbit, blurted out,

"Please don't cast a spell on us."

Dale and Mitchell both looked at her, confused. Then Mitchell burst out laughing.

"I won't. I'm not actually a magician. I told your class that so Rusty would think I would turn him into a frog if he tattled on you." Finley breathed a sigh of relief, and Mitchell continued, "By the way, congratulations. The two of you have gotten closer to a dangerous, very successful band of criminals in two weeks than I've been able to get in the past two years."

Finley stared at him, and Dale asked,

"What?"

Mitchell grinned.

"Now I'll tell you my story. Twelve years ago, a half-dozen local Michigan cemetery keepers started filing the same complaint with their police departments: Old graves were being disturbed with no explanation. No one seemed to think much of it, and the police departments tried to sweep the whole thing under the rug—after all, digging up a grave to investigate a claim like that is a fairly low-profile case that's complicated and expensive to pursue—but the complaints continued."

The list of complaints grew slowly but steadily, and finally the local departments took it to the state, and the state hired Mitchell Fitzwell, a Private Investigator, to look into them. After almost a year of unfruitful searching from Detroit, Mitchell temporarily moved from his home in Detroit to Malvern, the tiny town in north central Michigan. Malvern was smack in the middle of where most of the complains came from, but there were rarely disruptions in the actual town of Malvern, which would explain why David didn't think their suspicions merited investigation.

Mitchell had been living in Malvern for almost a year, working undercover as a school janitor and picking up other PI jobs. After eleven months with no real progress, he was considering returning to Detroit.

The diggers—it was rumored they called themselves The SODD, but Mitchell didn't really know—struck with no apparent rhyme or reason except that every month or two, another grave was disturbed. But with no real evidence beyond some dirt in the grass, he was powerless to unearth the bodies.

"Grave robbery is almost the perfect crime. If the crooks stay out of sight, there's practically no way to catch them. But now you've seen them in action. That's huge. With your word that they dug up Marv's grave, I should be able to get a warrant to disinter his body—well, his coffin, at least."

He frowned, fully aware that the missing body made this case much more serious, and even without Finley's word on the diggers, he could probably begin a real investigation based on that. He continued,

"For now, you two lay low. Finley, you need to tell the police about that note. We don't know what these people are capable of doing, but if they get caught they'll be looking at some serious consequences for how much they've stolen. So they really don't want to get caught." She nodded soberly, and he continued, "You also need to tell your mom about it.

In fact, I think I'll walk home with you and we can tell her together."

On their walk home, Finley peppered him with questions about being a PI, which he patiently answered. When they got home, she wasn't surprised to see that her mom's van wasn't in the driveway.

"She's not here."

"I don't mind waiting with you."

He sat down on the cement porch and Finley sat down next to him. After she ran out of questions for him, Mitchell asked her questions about herself. Before she realized it, she was telling him all about her life and her mom's good-for-nothing boyfriends and how her mom never knew where Finley was and never cared. She even told him how she'd hoped that catching the criminals would make her mom want to spend more time with her.

When Julie pulled into her driveway two hours later, she was surprised to see a strange man throwing a frisbee with her daughter.

She got out of the van and said,

"Who are you?"

"Mitchell Fitzwell. It's about Finley."

Assuming he was a teacher, Julie invited him in and told Finley to wait outside. Mitchell interjected.

"No, she needs to come too." Julie raised her eyebrows, and Mitchell continued. "I'm a private investigator, and I'm pretty sure that Finley's become involved in catching one of the largest crime syndicates in Michigan."

"Finley? With the whole graveyard thing? I thought that was over after last night."

Shaking his head, Mitchell said,

"It's not, but she might be the key to ending the whole thing."

"Oh." Julie looked at Finley, then said, "So, what do you want?"

Mitchell motioned for Finley to show her mother the note. Julie looked over it, then asked,

"This is real?"

"It is. Finley could be in danger. I'm going to tell the police so they can keep an eye on her, but it's important that you know where she is at all times."

Finley's mother looked guilty.

"All times?"

"Yes. Will that be a problem?"

Julie shuffled her feet.

"No, it should be fine."

Finley grinned at the prospect of her mother always knowing where she was. Mitchell went on.

"If we can catch them, Finley will be called upon to testify. That makes her extremely important to the case and extremely dangerous to them."

After a few more comments, Mitchell said,

"Well, it's nice to meet you. I'll be seeing you around, I'm sure." He handed her his card, and said, "Call me if you need anything or if anything happens." To Finley, he said, "Be extra observant about everything. Be very careful."

She nodded and he walked away, hands in his pockets, whistling. Julie hugged Finley close and said,

"Well, I guess we get to spend more time together. Should we make those cookies now?"

Finley nodded eagerly. They went to the store to get cookie ingredients and food for dinner. They prepared the cookie dough in silence, and it wasn't until the first batch was in the oven that Finley's mother said.

"I'm really sorry for everything." Finley shrugged. Her mother occasionally went through fits of reform, but they never lasted long. Even though Finley loved the idea of spending more time with her, she didn't want to get her hopes up. Her mother continued. "I promise I'll be better. This time, I really will."

After the cookies were finished, Julie made them dinner. She hadn't done that for a long, long time. They ate and watched a movie together. For the first time in weeks, Finley went to bed with a full heart.

Maybe it was all going to be okay after all.

14

ON SATURDAY MORNING, Finley woke up to the smell of pancakes. Her mother was rarely home on Saturday mornings, and when she was, she certainly didn't get up early or make breakfast. Maybe this was part of the new change. Finley eagerly bounced into the kitchen. It was going to be a good day.

After breakfast, Finley convinced her mom to come to the park with her. They swung on the swings for a long time, then laid in the grass watching the clouds.

After they'd been there for a long time, Finley sat bolt upright and said,

"Oh!"

Her mom sat up hastily.

"What's wrong?"

"It's Dean's birthday party today, and I promised him I would come, but I don't know what time it is. I hope I didn't miss it."

Finley's mom shrugged.

"It's probably okay if you did. I'm sure a lot of kids will go."

Finley frowned.

"I don't think so. He's new at school. I don't think he has many friends." She jumped to her feet. "The invitation is in my backpack. We need to go."

Her mother stood slowly, and the two of them hurried home. When they reached their porch, Finley's mom sank to the steps, breathing hard.

"Do you always run everywhere?"

Finley nodded.

"It's faster."

They went inside and Finley rummaged through her backpack, pulling out the crumpled envelope. She ripped it open and breathed a sigh of relief.

"It starts at one o'clock. I have just enough time to make him a card."

She ripped a piece of paper from one of her notebooks and drew Dean a picture of a monkey holding a baseball bat, with the caption, "Happy Birthday!" Then she went into her bedroom and looked around. There wasn't a lot to choose from—a few random odds and ends on the dresser, and a few special things in her junk drawer. After a moment of deliberation, Finley chose a ball of twine and an unused glow stick she'd gotten from the Fourth of July parade that summer. She clutched the paper, twine, and glow stick in her hand and went back out to the living room where her mom was sitting on the couch with the invitation in her hand.

"I'm going to come with you."

Finley was surprised, but not upset. She nodded.

"Let's go."

Dean's house was only a few blocks away from their house, and her mother made Finley walk the whole way there instead of running.

"It's not good manners to get to a birthday party out of breath."

When they arrived a few minutes after one o'clock, there were no cars in the driveway—but balloons were tied to the mailbox, and the garage doors were open. Tables inside the garage had confetti on them, and a sign on the porch that said, "Happy Birthday, Dean!"

Finley and her mother walked slowly up to the house, and Dean came running out to them.

"I knew you'd come! I told my mom you would come. I knew it."

His eyes looked suspiciously red behind his big glasses, but Finley didn't say anything. Instead, she grinned.

"Happy birthday! I didn't have time to wrap your present."

She thrust the twine, glow stick, and hand-made card at him. Dean took it, delighted.

"I lost my twine when we moved and I still haven't been able to find it." A short woman walked up behind him, and he held it up to show her. "Look, mom! New twine, to replace the stuff I lost!" She smiled and introduced herself to Finley's mother. Then she said,

"Dean, why don't you take Finley into the backyard and play some of the games?"

They went through the garage and into the back, where different yard games were set up, including a piñata and a beanbag toss game. As they threw beanbags, Finley asked,

"Where is everybody? I thought it started at one."

Dean nodded.

"It did."

"Oh."

Finley didn't say anything else, and after a few throws in silence, Dean asked what happened with Mitchell the day before. Finley told him all about it.

Their moms sat on chairs on the back deck watching them. After they'd played most of the games and she was still the only one there, Dale asked,

"Do you want a snack? My mom made taco dip. She was famous for it back in Greenville."

Finley nodded. She always wanted a snack. While they sat in the driveway eating chips and taco dip, Dean kept looking at his watch and sighing. Finally he said,

"Thanks for coming. I guess it was a silly idea to have a party. My mom said no one might come because I'm new. But I knew you would, because you said you would."

Finley smiled.

"It's never a silly idea to have a party. I never had one before, and I don't get invited to many. I liked it."

Dean grinned and wiped the last of his taco dip off his plate with his finger. Then he jumped up.

"Should we have cake now?"

Nodding, Finley stood. She followed him through the garage, to where their moms were sitting on the back porch. They'd discovered they had a lot in common, and Dean waited patiently until a lull in their conversation to ask for cake. It was a chocolate cake decorated with army men, and Dean's mom served them chocolate ice cream with it.

When Finley's mom came in from the back porch to tell Finley it was time to go, she cleaned up her plate and stood. Dean said,

"Thanks for coming."

Finley grinned.

"What are friends for?"

Dean flushed with joy, and said,

"I'll see you Monday."

As they walked home, Finley's mom said,

"He's very nice. How did you meet him?"

"Rusty was trying to steal his Twinkies."

Finley's mom frowned.

"Who's Rusty?"

A half-dozen moments flashed through her mind, but Finley only shook her head.

"Just a kid from school."

15

"IF I EVEN HEAR you squeak, you'll regret it."

Finley wondered how she could possibly squeak through the gag stuffed in her mouth. She blinked her eyes in the darkness of the paper bag, and moved her legs to brace herself for another turn when she heard the blinker clicking. The last time she'd tumbled down onto her side because she couldn't catch herself with her tied hands.

She was in the back of the Malvern Flower Shop delivery van, and Daisy was driving. Finley hadn't seen her face before today, but she recognized her voice. The van swung into a wide left turn, but this time Finley didn't topple over.

It had started out as a typical Monday—but as Finley ran down the sidewalk to school, it took an unexpected twist. A few blocks from school, a white van with flowers stenciled on it was parked in a driveway, blocking the sidewalk. As she approached, a smiling woman stepped around the side of the van holding a large bouquet of flowers. When she saw Finley, she called out,

"Oh, you're just what I needed!" Finley was almost even with the van. Without thinking, she stopped and replied,

"What?"

The woman shifted the flowers.

"I just have one more arrangement in the van, and I'm in such a hurry. Would you carry it inside for me? It'll just take a minute, and I'm sure it won't make you late for school."

For some reason the voice sounded familiar, but Finley couldn't quite place it. Without considering Mitchell's warning, she answered eagerly.

"Sure!"

She circled the van and looked through the open door, but she didn't see anything. The woman called to her,

"It's in the back, you'll have to climb in to get it!"

Sure enough, there were a few large boxes and an ornate bouquet close to the back door of the van. Finley jumped through the open van door and crawled over to the flowers, reaching for them—but as she did so, she heard the van door slide closed with a click. Finley, thinking it was a mistake, called out,

"Hey! I'm still in here!"

A dark form materialized from behind the large boxes and snickered.

"We know."

Suddenly, she knew why the woman's voice was familiar. It was Daisy, and this menacing voice belonged to Goofy. She tried to spin around and escape, but Goofy grabbed her shoulder and held it tightly while Daisy got in the driver's seat and backed the van out of the driveway. Goofy growled,

"The more trouble you make, the more trouble you'll be in."

He gagged her, put a brown paper bag over her head, and zip tied her hands behind her back. Finley sat there quietly, mind racing. She couldn't think of any good way to escape. After a short ride, they rolled to a stop. Finley heard Daisy jump out and Goofy open the door.

"Now, don't you make a scene."

Daisy called,

"All clear!" and Goofy pulled Finley's arm.

"Get out."

She stumbled onto the ground. Goofy took one arm and Daisy took the other, and they pulled her up a few steps, into a building, and up another flight of steps. Once they reached the top of the interior steps, Goofy pushed Finley into a chair and took the paper bag off her head. The chair was in the middle of a small, shadowy room with a stack of folding chairs in one corner and a few cardboard boxes stacked near the wall to her right. There was a closed door in front of her, across from the one they'd come through.

"You wait here. Pluto will be here later to deal with you."

They turned and walked out of the open door, talking to each other as they closed it. Daisy asked,

"What's he going to do to her?"

"Leave her there all day to scare her. Threaten her. I don't know, after that. Hopefully not much more . . ." His voice trailed off, then he said, "But you know Pluto when he gets angry. I guess we'll find out. We did our part, though. Let's get out of here."

Finley sat completely still for a few minutes, breathing deeply. It all happened so fast that she barely had time to be scared—but now, alone in the dim, dusty room, her heart was racing. Still gagged, she tried to yell but all that came out was a muffled yelp. Her previous confidence that no one would hurt her because she was "just a kid" started to disappear. If he was serious enough to kidnap her, there was no telling what else Pluto would do. Maybe he really would put her in the empty coffin.

Even though everyone had told her how dangerous these people were, she hadn't thought anyone was serious. But now she was tied and gagged and waiting for the ringleader. Maybe he would just threaten her and let her go home.

Finley tried not to think of any other possibilities, but the coffin kept coming to mind. She shuddered.

They hadn't tied her to the chair, so after a minute she jumped up and frantically rushed to the door they'd left through. To try the handle with her zip tied hands, she had to turn around and lift her hands awkwardly to the knob. It was locked.

Next, Finley used her toe to lift the lid of one of the boxes. It was full of papers. She walked over to the other door and tried the handle, grasping it behind her back.

To her surprise, it turned! Shouldering her way through the door, she gasped when she saw what was on the other side.

She was in the jewelry store! Everything was exactly the same as the last time she'd been there with Dale, except there were more footprints on the dusty floor. She hurried down the front stairs to the door and immediately groaned.

The door was deadbolted and the lock was higher than she could reach with her arms behind her back. After multiple failed attempts to turn the bolt, she sat down in frustration and stared at the door. Freedom was within reach, but she couldn't get to it. The words from the note raced through her mind:

We'll put you in the empty coffin.

She shivered and stood with renewed energy, trying again to reach the deadbolt. After a half-dozen more unsuccessful attempts, Finley started to cry. She slowly went back up the stairs and sat down in the chair, feeling completely defeated.

After a while, her tears subsided and she wondered what her mother would do when she found out Finley was gone. That made her start crying all over again.

But as the tears ran down her face unwiped, she remembered what Dale said about Jesus: Remember how I told you that you never have to be alone? Jesus really is with you and He really does love you, even though you can't see him.

Jesus still didn't make sense to Finley, and now she wished she'd asked Dale more questions. Maybe Jesus could have gotten her out of this mess. But one phrase Dale had said kept coming back to her: *You don't have to go to church to talk to Jesus.* She wiped her nose on her shoulder and said,

"Jesus, I don't know you and I don't understand you, but Dale says you know me. I'm scared. Please be with me like Dale says you're with him. I don't know what to do."

She waited quietly, wondering if she was supposed to hear something or see something—but she didn't. All that she felt was a tiny warmth seeping through her heart. Taking a deep breath, she rested her head on the back of the chair and closed her eyes.

Suddenly, Finley had an idea. Jumping up, she grabbed the chair, dragged it to the stairs, and awkwardly pulled it down behind her. At the small landing by the door, she stepped onto it.

It gave her exactly the height she needed, and this time she could easily reach the deadbolt. After sliding it into the unlocked position, she turned the handle. The door swung open. Finley leaped off her chair and rushed out of the building, with only one thing in mind: School. She had to find Mitchell.

A few people driving past saw the young girl running down the street with her arms behind her back and a rag wrapped around her mouth. One lady tried to stop her to ask if she was okay, but even when she yelled, Finley didn't look. She couldn't risk being stopped by anyone.

When Finley appeared in the office, bound and gagged, Mrs. Jackson jumped up.

"Are you all right?"

As soon as Mrs. Jackson took off the gag, Finley croaked, "I need to see Mitchell Fitzwell."

Mrs. Jackson looked at her curiously and paged Mitchell Fitzwell to the office. Moments later he appeared. When he saw Finley he smiled, but the smile dissolved quickly. There was red around her mouth from the tight gag, and he noticed the zip tie, scissors, and rag still in Mrs. Jackson's hands.

"What happened?"

"They kidnapped me."

They went into Mr. Munson's office where Finley hastily filled them both in on the whole situation, including Pluto's plan to come back later and "deal with her." By the time Finley was done talking, Mitchell had a plan.

They drove back to the jewelry store and parked down the street. Mitchell made a few calls, then they got out of the car. Finley wore the hood of her sweatshirt up as they went inside and into the small room.

Holding the gag in his hand, Mitchell asked,

"Are you sure you're okay with this? We might be able to figure out another way."

Finley nodded.

"I mean, it's all for a good cause, right? And you'll be right here the whole time?"

"Yes."

"Well, then I guess I'm fine with it."

After a brief pause, Mitchell said,

"You're a brave young woman."

He gagged Finley loosely and arranged the random boxes so he could hide behind them. He was silent, but Finley was trying to talk to Jesus more, so she kept whispering to him. The gag muffled her speech, but she figured it was clear enough.

"I have blonde hair, and I get in trouble a lot at school, and Dale is my best friend. He told me about you. I guess you know him?"

She paused, then went on to tell Him all about her mom, and Rusty, and school, and the night in the graveyard, and even the birthday party yesterday.

Suddenly, Mitchell's voice broke the silence. Finley jumped. Her nerves were on edge.

"Finley, who are you talking to?"

She answered sheepishly.

"Jesus."

"Oh."

She went back to her whispering, and Mitchell kept quiet. And they waited.

16

TIME MOVED IN SLOW motion. Finley had to pee. Every time she got up to stretch her legs, Mitchell quickly motioned for her to sit back down. If Pluto was suspicious at all, he might leave and they wouldn't be able to catch him.

After what felt like years, but was actually just most of one day, Finley heard a faint jingle of keys and heavy footsteps on the stairs. She kept her hands behind her and stared at the ground sullenly. The first voice she heard, to her surprise, was Goofy's.

"She's probably pretty scared."

She was relieved that Pluto wasn't alone. He grunted, and a moment later he opened the door. As soon as he saw her, he said,

"Finley Pike. You're nothing but trouble." She didn't look up. "You know something funny? I didn't even know who you were. I just dropped off a letter addressed for 'Finley' at the school and waited around long enough to hear the dumb secretary call you down. The rest was easy." A note of pride rang in his voice. "You're the brat who I've been seeing all over the place for the past week—even in my back yard with some snobby boy. That dumb kid gave away your name at the graveyard."

He paused, waiting for a reply. Finley frowned and said nothing, so he demanded,

"Now, tell me what you saw."

She remained silent. Mitchell had given her very specific instructions: If they wanted to get him on all the charges, Pluto had to admit to masterminding her kidnapping *and* robbing the grave. It would take some teasing out for him to flat out say it, though. Mitchell had said, "Whatever he says or asks, don't just answer right away. Repeat what he says. Ask questions back. Say you weren't there. Pretend you don't know what he's talking about."

She was remembering his instructions when Pluto spoke again.

"Come on, beanstalk. Get talking."

Daisy, standing behind Pluto with Goofy, chimed in,

"She can't talk around the gag, boss."

Pluto frowned and muttered under his breath. He moved toward Finley. She leaned away from him, but he grabbed her shoulder and used his other hand to untie the gag.

"Let's try again. What did you see?"

She looked at him with a blank expression, and said,

"What are you talking about? What did I see where?" Pluto huffed, but Finley continued, "Why did you kidnap me? I didn't do anything."

The look on his face was ugly.

"Don't lie to me, you little sneak. I know you were there."

Finley replied,

"Know I was where?"

They went through the same routine several times. Pluto was growing impatient. For the fifth time, he leaned toward her and, in a low, sinister voice, asked,

"Come on brat, what did you see at the graveyard?"

Finley saw her chance.

"Graveyard?"

Exasperated, Pluto took a step back.

"You know, on Thursday night when you hid in the graveyard and watched us."

She frowned. He had to say more than that.

"Watched you do what?"

He snorted.

"Get the biggest—"

But Goofy cleared his throat and said,

"Uh, boss?"

Pluto spun around.

"What?"

"What if she really wasn't there?"

Pluto bent down and put his face right in front of Finley's. His hot breath smelled like onions, and small beads of sweat stood out on his forehead. Finley didn't flinch, even when his low, gravelly voice scraped out another threat.

"Listen, pipsqueak. If you were there, the sooner you admit it the better it will be for you. If you weren't there, maybe we'll let you go. So you may as well just tell us."

Finley tilted her chin up with the same obstinate defiance that was constantly earning her time in detention.

"I already said I wasn't there."

Pluto narrowed his eyes.

"I don't believe you."

She shrugged.

"So what difference does it make what I say?"

Daisy and Goofy shuffled uneasily behind Pluto. He'd led them to believe that this girl could land them all in jail—but she seemed innocent to them. They began to think about the consequences if they were caught kidnapping her.

Goofy spoke again.

"Boss, I think she might be telling the truth."

Shaking his head adamantly, Pluto said,

"She's not. There are too many coincidences for her not to have been there."

Finley, seeing an opportunity in Pluto's rising anger, chimed in.

"Not have been where? The graveyard?"

Pluto wasn't a patient man to begin with, and between Goofy's reluctance and Finley's stubbornness, he was losing his cool. With this impudent question, he burst.

"Yes! At the graveyard on Thursday when we were digging up Marv Jacobsen, you little twerp!"

She looked at him with big, shocked eyes, and Daisy groaned. Finley didn't miss a beat.

"Why would you do that?"

"To steal his gold, you idiot."

Daisy pleaded from behind him,

"Boss, you said you just wanted to scare her. Now you're going to have to . . ." Her voice trailed off. It was one thing to steal from dead people, but to harm a child? Goofy added his two cents.

"I didn't sign up for this. I don't want to go to jail. She's just a kid."

Pluto snorted and turned toward Goofy and Daisy.

"You won't go to jail. No one will ever know it was us."

Goofy wasn't convinced.

"But I'm sure they'll look for her, and what if they connect Daisy and I to her kidnapping? Someone could have seen us."

"You worry too much."

Finley was beginning to wonder how long Mitchell would wait. She thought he had everything he needed, but he still hadn't appeared. Maybe he wanted to hear it one more time. She whispered, "Jesus, please help," then cleared her throat loudly and asked,

"Let me get this straight. You stole from a dead guy?"

Pluto didn't even turn around to face her. At this point, it didn't matter what she knew.

"Yes, we did. What's the big deal? He doesn't need his money. He's dead."

Goofy and Daisy both cringed in discomfort, but suddenly their eyes went wide with real dread. Mitchell had stood up behind the boxes. They were in a triangle—Finley as one point, Mitchell as another, and Daisy, Goofy, and Pluto as the third. With his back to Mitchell, Pluto grunted.

"What's the matter with you two? You look like you saw Marv's ghost."

Goofy pointed, and Daisy stuttered,

"M-m-maybe we did."

As Pluto slowly turned, Mitchell said,

"I'm certainly not a ghost. The three of you are under arrest for theft and kidnapping."

Goofy and Daisy stood quietly, but Pluto wasn't convinced.

"Says who?"

Daisy whispered,

"Pluto, he's got a gun."

Pluto kept up his cavalier air.

"I'm not just believing any idiot with a gun."

Mitchell grinned, but his voice was far from friendly.

"I think you'd better believe me. Let's go."

He motioned toward the steps with his gun, and Pluto, realizing he meant business, reluctantly stepped toward them. Goofy and Daisy followed quietly, as Pluto railed at his accomplices.

"I knew the two of you were incompetent. What did you mess up? How did he get here?"

Goofy said,

"Maybe he was already here and we just didn't see him. Maybe he's homeless and was sleeping here."

Daisy giggled nervously and added,

"Yeah. We did exactly what you told us to do. How could it be our fault? It was your idea."

They were stomping down the stairs now, and Pluto asked,

"A homeless guy with a gun? Right. This isn't my fault, you nincompoop. Did you check all the doors?" Neither responded, and Pluto groaned. "Last time I ever work with knuckleheads."

Mitchell replied,

"It's going to be the last time you work with anybody for a very long time."

They traipsed down the stairs and out into the street, Finley a few steps behind everyone else. It was dusk, and a half-dozen state police cars lined the narrow alley. Pluto, Daisy, and Goofy were immediately put into handcuffs and assisted into squad cars. Mitchell talked to the police officers, and Finley stood by him quietly, until suddenly she heard someone yell.

"FINLEY!"

Dale and his parents and Finley's mom were standing at the end of the line of police cars. Finley ran toward them, and Dale met her half way and enveloped her in a massive hug.

"I was so worried about you. When you didn't come to school I thought maybe something went wrong and I told Mr. Slinch but I don't know if he did anything about it but then Mrs. Jackson called me down to the office and told me everything and how you were going back with Mitchell and I thought that was *so cool*."

There was a tiny spark of envy in his voice. Finley grinned.

"Thanks, Dale."

They walked back across the street to their parents, and Finley's mom took Finley into her arms.

"I was so worried about you."

She was crying.

"Thanks, mom."

"I'm never going to let you out of my sight again, if I can help it. Awful things could have happened to you . . ."

Her voice trailed off, but Finley grinned.

"It's okay, mom. I'm okay."

They hugged for a long time. After that they went down to the police station so Finley could give all the details of her side of the story, including her testimony regarding everything Pluto said to her in the jewelry store. Then they went to the grocery store and bought ingredients for spaghetti, which they made for dinner.

It was the best spaghetti Finley had ever eaten.

17

THE NEXT DAY, Mitchell stopped Finley, Dale, and Dean in the hallway as they were leaving school. He looked at Finley and Dale and asked,

"Do you two have a few minutes?"

Finley motioned at Dean.

"He knows all about it. Can he come too?"

Mitchell nodded. He led them to his janitor's closet, where he'd explained the SODD to Finley and Dale just a few days earlier. It felt like so long ago. He said,

"Pluto gave a full confession. I thought you might want to hear his story."

The children nodded.

"Twelve years ago, Ronald Jackson was working at the factory and living in the trailer park behind the summer drive-in. He was barely making enough to support his family, he hated his job, and above all, he hated being poor. Then one day, he heard a strange rumor. Old Mrs. Smitty, who died a year before, had been buried wearing every single piece of her gold and diamond jewelry. Added up, it was all worth at least fifty thousand dollars. It would take Ronald a year and a half to make that at the factory."

They listened closely as Mitchell continued.

"Ronald came up with a plan to dig up Mrs. Smitty's grave and take her jewelry, but he knew he couldn't do it alone. So, he got his two best friends, Miranda Swale and Tim Jones, in on it, and it went off without a hitch. He pawned the jewelry, gave Miranda and Tim both a cut of the profits, and pocketed the rest."

Mitchell explained that it was the first in a long string of robberies orchestrated by Ronald Jackson, alias Pluto. Before long, the Malvern group had grown to five members. Over the years, as members of his team moved to different cities, they started their own SODDs, which stands for Society of Digging Dandelions. He continued,

"The different regional SODDs help each other dig. That's why you saw so many people at the graveyard, Finley. Malvern's team is only five people. All over Michigan, more than 300 graves have been robbed in the past twelve years. But thanks to the two of you, we can put away the man who started it all, Ronald Jackson, also known as Pluto. And two of the other original members, Miranda and Tim, who you might know better as Minnie and Mickey."

Finley's eyes were wide, and Dale said,

"Whoa."

Dean pushed his glasses up his nose in amazement.

"Finley, you don't have to be afraid of any of them. Pluto turned in the other members of his team in exchange for a shorter sentence. I don't know what he was like when he started this whole business, but after years of robbing graves, I think his conscience is rock hard. He'll be away for a long time, considering that he was behind your kidnapping and when we arrested him he was armed."

Finley shivered at the thought of what could have happened if she hadn't escaped. After a few more details, Mitchell added,

"But what I really wanted to tell you both is that today is my last day here. Tomorrow I'm going back to Detroit. We might have enough evidence to convict the members of the other SODDs, if we can get their names. It probably won't happen all at once, but it's a start."

They exchanged goodbyes. As he hugged Finley, he said, "You're a very brave young woman."

Mitchell watched the children walk down the hallway. He hadn't told them about the brewing case and mystery surrounding the missing body. He suspected it was something much more serious than a ring of grave robbers, and he didn't want Finley to get involved again.

When the three children got outside into the bright, brisk afternoon, they grinned at each other. Even though it had only been exactly two weeks since that first fateful day in the jewelry store, it felt like years ago.

Dale spoke first, with a twinkle in his eye.

"I think it's a new chapter, folks." Dean and Finley nodded, as he continued, "Yesterday afternoon I explored the old abandoned laundromat. I could show you guys if you want?"

Dean said,

"Cool! Yeah!"

But Finley shook her head vehemently, and Dale laughed. Finley replied,

"I have to be home for dinner. We're making meatloaf. But we could go to Dale's house and get a snack, then go to the park?"

They took off running toward Dale's house. It felt nice to have things back to normal, and to have Dean along. Little did either of them know how valuable he would prove to be in the future.

At the park, Finley told the two boys about every single detail of being kidnapped. Even with all her details, they kept stopping her with questions. When she got to the part about sitting alone in the jewelry shop before escaping, Dean asked,

"Weren't you scared?"

She nodded.

"So scared. But then I remembered what Dale told me." Dale looked confused. "You know, about Jesus loving me and always being with me and how I could talk to him anywhere."

"Oh. Yeah."

Stopping her swing, she looked at him seriously.

"So I talked to him. And he helped me." An enormous grin lit up Dale's face, and Finley continued. "And then once I started, I didn't want to stop. So when I came back and was sitting up there with Mitchell for hours, I told him all about myself."

Dean asked,

"Mitchell?"

Dale laughed.

"No, Jesus."

"Oh."

Dale was still laughing, and Finley frowned at him.

"Why are you laughing?"

"Jesus already knows you. He created you, remember? I told you that."

Finley shrugged.

"I still don't really understand, it all. But I wanted to tell Him, just the same."

Dale nodded.

"Yeah, that makes sense."

Dean, who had been listening closely, asked,

"Who's Jesus? How could he have made us? My parents always tell me that they made me."

Dale grinned and started,

"Well, it's like this—" But before he could say more, he interrupted himself. "Guys, look. Do you feel like that car is driving past that house really slow? This is the third time it has gone by."

Finley looked at the rusty purple car and frowned.

"That's weird."

"Let's see if we can get closer."

Inside the car, a man and a woman closely watched the large house across the street. The man, a skinny, sniveling fellow, said,

"See? They leave the house around this time every day, and don't come back till at least seven. We'd have plenty of time to get in, get what we wanted, and get out."

The woman spoke around the cigarette dangling from her lips.

"Sounds good, Larry. Tomorrow?"

The man nodded. Finley, Dale, and Dean were walking toward the car, and he turned.

"Let's go before those lousy kids come over here and bug us. I hate kids."

The children watched the car slowly roll away, and Finley said,

"It's probably nothing."

Dale nodded reluctantly.

"Yeah. Probably."

He studied the license plate of the car, and Dean asked,

"But what if it's not?"

Curious about what Dale started to tell Dean and Finley about Jesus? Here's what he would have said:

Dale grinned and started,

"In the beginning, when God created the world, there was no sin. Then the Devil caused Adam and Eve to sin."

Dean interrupted.

"You mean like my next-door neighbor, Adam?"

"No, Adam was the first man. God created him a few thousand years ago. They were perfect when God made them, then they sinned. Because they sinned, they couldn't live with God forever. But that made God really sad. He wanted us to live with Him, but He couldn't stand our sins. So He sent His Son, Jesus, to the earth. Jesus is also God."

Dean scratched his head, and Finley laughed.

"See?! I'm not the only one who thinks it's confusing."

Dale nodded, and Dean said,

"I'll finish quick, then you can ask all the questions. Jesus came to earth and died to pay for our sins in God's sight, because every person who sins has to die. But because Jesus didn't sin, he couldn't stay dead. So he rose from the grave. And now, if you want a relationship with Jesus, you just have to admit that you sinned, believe that Jesus died on the cross for those sins and God raised Him from the dead, confess him as the king of your life, and live your life from then on to please Him. Then you'll go to heaven to live with Him when you die!"

Dean asked,

"I guess it's confusing, but it's also kind of simple."

Finley nodded, and Dale replied,

"Yep. It is. Race you to the other side of the field!"

CPSIA information can be obtained
at www.ICGtesting.com
Printed in the USA
LVHW081321211121
704028LV00014B/1851